DEAD STREAM

MAR ROMASCO-MOORE

VIKING

VIKING

An imprint of Penguin Random House LLC

1745 Broadway, New York, New York 10019

First published in the United States of America by Viking,
an imprint of Penguin Random House LLC, 2025

Visit us online at PenguinRandomHouse.com.

Library of Congress Cataloging-in-Publication Data is available.

ISBN 9780593691885

1st Printing

Printed in the United States of America

LSCC

Edited by Jenny Bak

Design by Lucia Baez | Text set in CG Times

The authorized representative in the EU for product safety and compliance is Penguin
Random House Ireland, Morrison Chambers, 32 Nassau Street, Dublin D02 YH68, Ireland,
https://eu-contact.penguin.ie.

DEAD STREAM

 Brick is live now with 33.5K viewers
Category: Just Chatting
I DO WHATEVER CHAT TELLS ME—10K SUB SPECIAL

Brick, a basic white guy wearing a tan sweatshirt emblazoned with his own username, is sitting at his desk. He has been streaming for twenty-seven minutes.

> "Oh hey, thanks for the raid, KingCoal. Welcome, KingCoal viewers! Welcome to the Brick House."

Chat
[27:07]—raid let's go <3 <3 <3
[27:07]—RAID
[27:08]—KingCoal says HIIIII

> "If you're just joining, here's the deal. I've got donations turned on, twenty-dollar minimum, and I have to do anything they tell me. Anything!"

He leans close to the camera. His face blurs.

For a moment the background of the room comes into focus. Behind him, a bookcase made of white cubes, each cube full of artfully arranged memorabilia. To the right: a cream-colored leather sofa, with a stack of rust-red rectangular throw pillows. To the left: a door, closed.

"I am your puppet, chat. I am your puppet!"

> [27:22]—WOOOOO
> [27:22]—catjam
> [27:23]—anything?? Sounds dangerous

Though a bright light is focused on Brick's face, the rest of the room is dim, lit only by a large neon sign on the wall behind him— the looping glass tubes shaping the letters of Brick's username. He leans back, pulls the adjustable arm of his Shure SM7B microphone with pop filter and cloud lifter closer to his face.

> "Well okay, almost anything. Nothing that violates terms of service, obviously, and nothing that's going to cost more than like a hundred bucks in one go. Unless you donate a hundo and then, shit, who knows. Feel free to try it and find out."

He grins, pushes an unruly hank of floppy brown hair out of his eyes. He's got a boyish energy, always moving in some way, even as he remains seated in his high-backed gaming chair.

> [27:37]—I'm broke someone donate for me
> [27:38]—Ten month sub, I love you Brick

"All right, let's see what you monsters are going to make me do next. Mods, send the next one through."

Text appears in the center of the screen. A robotic voice reads it out in a steady monotone.

> **Crafty_Cha0s_ donated $20: Dump your water bottle on your head**

Brick holds his water bottle up to the camera. It's part of his limited-edition merch line, with his name on the side. He pulls an exaggerated face of mock fear, eyes wide, teeth gritted.

"Well, I guess this one was inevitable."

He makes a big show of tilting the bottle slightly, flinching, hesitating.

[28:03]—hydro homies
[28:04]—come on
[28:04]—omg do it already

He chuckles, eyes fixed somewhere to the left of the camera. His second monitor, where he can read the chat.

"Okay, fine, fine, here goes."

He upends the nearly full bottle. Water streams down his face, plastering his hair to his forehead.

> [28:11]—omegalul
> [28:11]—he looks like cat gettin bath

"Aw, shit."

Brick jumps up, knocks the camera askew. We see the corner of his desk as he pushes his rainbow-LED optical switch keyboard out of the way and mops up the spilled water with a wadded T-shirt—also from his merch line.

> [28:21]—F for Brick's keyboard
> [28:22]—RIP

Brick sits back down, adjusts the camera. He wraps the T-shirt around his damp hair like a towel.

"Crisis averted. It was touch and go for a moment there, but I think the patient will pull through."

He holds up his keyboard, mimes rocking it like a baby. The robotic voice speaks again, awkwardly sounding out an unpronounceable username.

Tjbnfskha donated $25: Open the door

Brick squints at his second monitor.

"Open my door? There's nothing that exciting out there, chat, I swear."

> [28:50]—door?
> [28:51]—lol why
> [28:51]—weirdchamp

"But sure, whatever, I'll open my door for you. Does that sound dirty? I mean, I know you, chat. You can make anything dirty. I've seen the fan edits. There's some real out-of-pocket shit out there. Well, I said I'd do anything, so . . . "

He bounces up from his seat, gives the camera a double thumbs-up and a salute. His makeshift T-shirt towel falls off. He saunters to the door.

> [29:12]—he's calling us out
> [29:12]—Brick, i've had a really rough month . . . your streams are the only thing that makes me feel okay anymore

The camera shifts focus from foreground to background. Brick's voice is muffled.

"Okay, I'm opening it. Wow, can you see that, chat? So thrilling! A hallway."

There is indeed a hallway. It is shadowy, indistinct.

> [29:24]—hallway reveal!
> [29:24]— <3 <3 <4

Brick returns. The camera settles back into focus on his face as he plops into his chair.

"Well, I hope that viewer was satisfied with how they spent their twenty-five dollars. No refunds, boys! Any new viewers, this is the kind of action-packed content that you can depend on here. Hallways for days. Absolute pinnacle of entertainment. Worth a sub, right? Worth a prime, at least."

The hallway is dark. Out of focus.

"Aw, hey, AvenueB, thanks for the twenty gifted subs!"

Something moves out there.

> [29:50]—I just resubbed for 3 months
> [29:51]—wait wtf
> [29:51]—what is that?

The thing in the hallway is indistinct, blurry. It's hard to say at first if it is moving toward us or away.

> [29:58]—omg behind you
> [29:59]—BRICK look behind you

No, it is moving closer. A shadow. The height of a person. The shape of a person.

"Okay, people are saying to look behind me."

Brick looks.

"There's nothing there."

But we can see it. There, in the doorway. The shape of a head, a neck, shoulders. It is too dark to make out a face.

> [30:05]—do you guys see that
> [30:05]—yeah there's someone there
> [30:05]—omfg

Brick turns back to us. He laughs.

"Chat, stop fucking with me."

He glances over at his second monitor, startles. He looks quickly from screen to door and back. "That's . . . Okay. Huh."

[30:18]—is this part of a game or something?

"Chat, it's just some kind of visual glitch."

[30:21]—this is freaking me out for real

"There's nothing there. That's just on the screen. Maybe it's a problem with the software."

Brick stands up and approaches the door. As he nears it, the figure shifts backward into the hallway.

[30:33]—omg no
[30:33]—NO NO

Brick closes the door, returns to his desk. He looks at the monitor to the left for a long time. He's more still than he's been this whole stream, face slack as he types, concentrating on something we can't see.

[30:49]—he didn't see it?
[30:50]—brick what was that

Finally, apparently satisfied, he snaps back into character: grinning, animated. He tries to run his hand through his hair, discovers it is still damp.

"Okay, let's get the next dono up on the screen, see what else you maniacs have in store for me."

[31:07]—the door!!

Behind him, the door is opening. He doesn't seem to notice.

"Mods? Send the next one through."

[31:19]—forget about donations and look behind you
[31:20]—Brick!!
[31:20]—brick the door the door

sixtynine420 donated $20: for f*ck's sake man look behind you!!!!

Brick laughs.

"Seems like this one came through too late. But sure, okay. Anything for you, my good sir sixtynine420."

He makes a face, does a big, dramatic turn.

"Nope, nothing there. Door is closed. All is well."

On the screen, the door is open. It is clearly open.

[31:47]—what is he talking about?
[31:47]—the door is open!

The figure is framed in the doorway. The shadowy shape of a person.

[31:48]—chat calm down he's clearly doing a bit
[31:48]—I AM SCARED

Brick turns back to us, grinning, nonchalant.

Abruptly, the neon sign goes out. The ring light that we cannot see—the one behind the camera, pointing at Brick—goes out too.

[31:57]—OMG
[31:57]—brick wtf

The room is plunged into darkness. The focus reels, the camera fuzzing in and out.

[31:59]—is this real?????

Brick's face is only barely visible now, illuminated by his screen's bluish glow. His eyes shift to the monitor on the left.

"Okay, what? That's weird. I swear this stream is so scuffed."

He looks behind him.

There is something moving in the darkness. A blurred shape. A shadow.

[32:04]—im literally shaking rn
[32:05]—can everyone else see that?

Brick looks back at the second monitor, frowning.

"The lights are still on, chat. I don't know why it's showing up like that on the screen. In real life, in my room, the lights are—"

The shadow moves suddenly. Rushing forward. Reaching.

[32:16]—BRICK
[32:16]—brick! behind you!
[32:16]—oh god

1://

The internet is a graveyard. Full of broken links. Inactive forums. Unloadable images. Ghost traffic from automated processes churning out useless data. The social media profiles of the dead.

Teresa refreshes the page. She refreshes it again. And again.

In the upper-left corner: the same picture of Becks, as always. Wry smile. Bangs askew. Her hand a blur as she reaches up to brush them out of her eyes. At the top of the page, her full name: Rebecca Crenley.

Beneath it, her last post.

> May 27 at 1:26 AM
>
> Ah yes the high-pitched squealing of the spinny plate in my broken microwave when I try to heat a mug of water that shit is my JAM

Such a silly post, and yet every word of it is burned into Teresa's memory now. She's read it at least once every day for the past year.

Teresa refreshes. The page blinks away and then back, the same as before. Becks's smile, her last post. No hint of what was going to happen.

On her worst days, Teresa just sits here, refreshing over and over, staring so hard at the picture of Becks she can almost imagine it is moving, almost imagine it is gazing back.

Her therapist says this is an unhealthy coping mechanism, but Teresa can't bring herself to stop. She is addicted to that infinitesimal moment of hope each time the page reloads. Maybe this time it will be different. Maybe this time something will change.

But it never does. It never will. Becks is gone. She isn't coming back.

Teresa pushes back from her computer, rolls her desk chair over to the window. The oak tree in neighbor #2's yard catches the glow of the evening sun, soaring branches painted with orange light.

It's been almost two months now since Teresa last went outside.

Four months since she went any farther than her own backyard.

Across the alleyway, neighbor #3 is letting out their dog. Squirrels zip along the power lines like an extra current. A V of geese knifes into view overhead. Teresa's phone dings.

A notification: Brick has just gone live.

Teresa turns away from the real window to the other window, the better window. Through this one she can see not just a few backyards but the whole world. She pulls up Brick's stream on her laptop, which she's configured as a second monitor, and starts a screen recording. On her primary monitor, she opens her video editing software, ready in case she wants to make a clip. The "stream starting soon" screen gives way to Brick's face.

"Hello, boys," he thunders, grinning into the camera, positively bursting with energy drink exuberance. "Today is a very special day. We did it! We hit thirty thousand subscribers."

A sharp knock. Teresa jumps, spins around just in time to see her bedroom door creaking open.

"Hey, honey," her mother says, poking her head around the doorframe. "Am I interrupting?"

Teresa's parents won't let her put a lock on her door. She'd been asking since before the accident, but it's taken on a new importance now. She's tried to explain that it's partially for their own good. What if she's streaming? Do they really want to be suddenly exposed to a bunch of internet strangers? Her mother said she'd just knock first.

Teresa pulls off her headphones. "I guess not."

"You coming down to dinner tonight?"

This is a formality more than a real question. Her mother's tone makes it clear that she already knows the answer. Is already disappointed.

"Not tonight," says Teresa. It has been six days since she last went downstairs.

Her mother pushes the door farther open, steps all the way inside the room. Teresa tenses. She hates that anyone can barge in at any time. She'd feel so much safer with a lock.

"Can you try, honey?" her mom says. "I think it would mean a lot to Jason. He had a tough day at school today."

Teresa doesn't answer. She is gritting her teeth. Her anxiety is rising, a faint but persistent hum. She wants her mom to leave. She wants to be alone.

Her mom is wrong, anyway. Jason, her little brother, doesn't want to see her. She supposes they'd been growing apart for a while, even before the accident, but in the last few weeks he hasn't spoken a single word to her. If they pass in the hallway, he ignores her, glaring down at the floor. Two days ago, he had a friend over after school. She overheard them in the hallway as they walked by her door. The friend had asked, "Is that your sister's room?"

Jason's reply: "I don't have a sister."

"Who's that?" her mom asks, gesturing at Teresa's computer.

"Brick."

"Oh. Is he one of your friends?"

Teresa rolls her eyes. "No."

She's told her mom who Brick is—the first streamer she ever watched, the one who inspired her to start making her own content. She's also told her mom the names of the friends she streams with—Ozma, Jolley, Pete45, RnBw, Sparklekitty—and shown her pictures of them, but her mom insists she can't keep "all those internet people" straight. She doesn't quite see them as real, Teresa suspects. It's funny—sometimes they seem more real to Teresa than anyone else.

Her mother leans against the doorframe. She looks like she is getting comfortable, like she intends to stay and chat. "What's he doing?" she asks.

Teresa glances back at her desk. Her setup isn't exactly fancy—an old dusty tower and monitor, plus a laptop beside it. The laptop was a birthday gift from her parents a few months back. She's pretty sure they were hoping its portability would encourage her to spend more time out of the house. Instead, she's used it to go further inward.

On the laptop screen, Brick is speaking, though there's no sound, his voice lost in the headphones sitting on the desk. Teresa reaches over, slams the laptop shut, a little more aggressively than she meant to. "Nothing," she says.

Her mother looks hurt. She opens her mouth, seems about to protest, then waves her hand, a slight gesture, as if brushing something away. "Well, I'll make a plate for you then."

She heads back downstairs. The minute she's out of sight, Teresa jumps up and closes her door. Not quite a slam. But firmly shut.

She leans against the door, takes a deep breath, feeling a mix of guilt and relief. Her mother means well. She's just trying to help. But she doesn't understand.

Teresa needs to be alone. She needs to be in her bedroom, with the door shut. Lately, that's the only way she feels safe. She can keep everything clean, keep everything under control. Nothing can hurt her and, just as important, she can't hurt anyone else.

Teresa returns to her desk, reopens the laptop, slips her headphones on. She missed a little of the stream, so hopefully nothing major happened. She hits the record button again.

She is seeing Brick through a screen of course, from a great distance, but he truly does seem more real to her, in a way, than her own mother. More vivid. There is something about him. His energy, his easy laugh.

It's like he fits into his own skin better than other people fit into theirs. Better than Teresa does, certainly. She'd always felt uneasy in her body, disconnected from it, a reluctant inhabitant.

She pulls up a video she needs to edit on her other monitor, glancing over occasionally at Brick's stream as she works. In addition to livestreaming, Teresa runs three separate video channels: one for short clips of more popular creators, one for the recorded VODs of her own streams, and one for video essays analyzing streaming trends.

Onstream, Brick dumps a water bottle over his head, wetting his hair. Is that worth cutting out and posting to her clip channel?

His viewers get possessive about his hair. It's dark brown and goes wavy when it grows out. Many fans were upset when he cut it about a month ago. Teresa had seen "in memoriam" fan art, half joking, of course, but also half-serious.

Even she'd had a moment of dismay when she tuned in to the first stream after he chopped it off. Brief discomfort at the change, the unfamiliarity, like a child who doesn't recognize their father after he shaves his beard.

A lot of the viewers also have raging crushes on Brick, of course. Teresa doesn't, but she understands. She wouldn't want to date him, but she often thinks she'd like to be him.

He is handsome, confident, enthusiastic, fun. He has the most contagious laugh. It starts small and then expands, like it is opening its arms to all fifty thousand people watching, to gather them in. To let you in.

In on the joke. In on his life. Into his bedroom every day.

He is opening his bedroom door onstream now. Teresa decides she will make a clip of him getting his hair wet. She ports the footage into her editing software, scrubs back to find the right moment.

Her phone buzzes. A text from her friend Ozma.

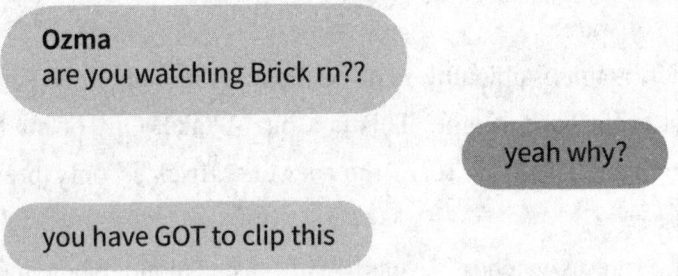

Ozma
are you watching Brick rn??

yeah why?

you have GOT to clip this

Teresa's eyes return to the stream. Brick is sitting in his chair again, chatting away, gesturing enthusiastically. Nothing out of the ordinary.

And then she sees it.

In the hallway, through the open door.

She jolts back so hard, her chair rolls away from the desk. She has to laugh at herself then, though her heart is pounding. It just startled her, that's all. A jump scare. She hates those.

She leans back in, squinting at the indistinct figure standing in the doorway behind Brick. He's obviously set this up himself. Clever. It's a cardboard cutout, she'd bet on it. She knows he owns several. Sometimes he'll arrange them in the room behind him and talk to them during his stream. One is Danny DeVito. This figure is too tall for that. Perhaps it's The Rock?

And then it moves.

She doesn't jolt back this time, but her stomach drops. It couldn't be a genuine intruder, right? A housebreaker, caught on camera? A crazed fan who'd tracked him down?

She hasn't been paying attention to what Brick is saying, but she tunes back in now. He is claiming there's a glitch. Saying the figure isn't there in real life, but only on the stream, the screen, the broadcasting software.

Which is impossible unless he set up an elaborate green screen, so he must be in on it. Right? This is a bit. A fake. One of his friends, lurking there, trying to scare the viewers. Brick is only pretending not to see.

Still, Teresa watches, riveted. She gasps aloud when the lights go off. The figure moves forward. Somehow it grows no clearer as it approaches the light of the screen. The face remains a smudge of shadowy pixels, the body a mere silhouette, out of focus and barely distinguishable from the darkness of the room. The figure reaches out a hand toward Brick's back. Does it touch him? It's too hard to see in the gloom, but Brick goes suddenly rigid in his chair, face frozen in an expression of shock.

The stream ends abruptly, which startles Teresa almost as much as the figure appearing. Brick never ends stream without his signature outro: "Alrighty, boys, subscribe to me everywhere and together we'll build this house, brick by brick!" Weird. She'll want to check the fan server and social media, see what everyone is saying.

But first—

She's done it so many times the actions are muscle memory now. Pulling the footage, cutting it down.

It's not real, she thinks, as she picks out a screenshot for the thumbnail. Not a real stranger. Not a real threat. Brick is in on it. If it was real, she wouldn't do this. Of course she wouldn't. That would cross a line. It would be invasive, parasitic, like those people who post clips of strangers getting hurt, trying to profit off someone else's pain.

But it's not real, so this is fine.

She posts the clip.

 **WhomegaLil is live now with 1.7K viewers**
Category: Battle Game
RANKING UP TODAY DIAMOND TIER OR BUST

WhomegaLil—"Lil" for short—is a young Korean American woman wearing a tank top and a long pastel-pink wig.

She's down in the right corner of the screen. Her room is lit purple and pink with recessed LED tubes. More light comes from a glass-fronted minifridge displaying cans of Lyte-Vorb energy drinks, one of her sponsors.

"Oh, fuck that. What is this damage?"

Most of the screen is taken up by the game she's playing, a chaos of tiny, fast-moving units, turret guns, and bright lights. Lil frowns with concentration.

Chat
[23:11]—hello lil im a new viewer
[23:11] <3 LiL
[23:12]—ur game is off today lil

"That is so broken how much damage she just did. Is that—aw, hell!"

The screen grays out. Lil has been slain.

[23:17]—nt
[23:18]—WAYTOODANK
[23:18]—LMAO

She sits back with a sigh, minimizes the game. Clicks something. The small square of her room in the corner expands to fill the screen. She spins her white-and-pink gamer chair around, grabs an energy drink from her minifridge, pops it open.

"Maybe I should go back to playing as an assassin. That was a decent match until the very end, though. I feel like I should have had that."

[23:32]—F
[23:32]—F
[23:32]—o7
[23:33]— F

"Don't F me, chat. Get those out of the chat. I don't want to see those."

[23:38]—LULW
[23:38]—F

"Thanks for the six months, SeaNovaGalaxy. And the fourteen from Crystal896!"

[23:44]—did u see the brick clip??

[23:44]—F for brick

"What clip? Clip of Brick?"

She types something in a window we can't see, seems to be considering what she finds.

[23:50]—Watch it on stream
[23:50]—yeah do it

"Fine, fine, I'll watch it."

She clicks and a new window appears on-screen, showing the clip of Brick's stream. The events from earlier that evening play out. Brick gets up. He opens the bedroom door.

[25:20]—brick + lil 4eva <3 <3
[25:21]—omg are they dating?

"Is he going to fall down or something? What am I watching this for?"

[25:42]—they would be such a cute couple
[25:42]—wait for it
[25:43]—ugh yes so cute

"And for the millionth time, chat, *no*! We're not a couple, we're just friends. Get off my dick about—"

She sees it, then. The figure in the doorway. She jumps.

"Goddamn it, chat, what the hell is that?"

> [26:16]—I saw this live and it scared me
> [26:17]—it's a ghost

The clip ends. Lil laughs, though it doesn't sound quite genuine.

> [27:05]—lil do you know anything about this? Is brick ok???
> [27:06]—maybe you should call him
> [27:06]—RIP brick

Lil rewinds the clip, pauses just after the figure first appears.

"Wow, yeah, he really got me. I guess I'll DM him just to make sure he's not murdered. God, that's"— she laughs again, more easily this time—"genius, you know. That's just genius. Calm down, chat, he's probably fine. I'll let you know if he replies."

> [27:34]—lil is simpin for brick
> [27:34]—hey Lil its my birthday today

She stares down at her phone for a while, silent. A small animated banner runs across the bottom of the screen: "Partnered with Lyte-Vorb. Use code WHOMEGALIL for 10% off."

"He's probably asleep. He's got a ridiculous sleep schedule. Look, though, he's trending after this stunt. That boy knows how to promote himself."

[27:56]—she got it bad
[27:57]—clout chaser

"No, chat, I'm not clout chasing. Jesus Christ, why are you all the worst?"

[28:05]—we are trash it is true

Lil takes a long glug of her energy drink, then grins at the camera.

"You know I hate every single one of you. On an individual level. Passionately. Now enough of this react-Andy bullshit, chat. Let's get back to the game."

[28:30]—its ok we hate u too lil
[28:30]—<3

2://

Teresa checks her phone first thing after she wakes up.

That clip of Brick—the one with the shadowy figure appearing behind him—has been doing serious numbers. It's outperforming all her other clips, click-through rate high, view count well into the ten thousands and climbing steadily. A lot of eyes.

Teresa feels a nervous energy buzzing up inside her.

The good kind, though. The exciting kind. Like the buzzing of her phone—a new notification, that little burst of pleasure, novelty, anticipation. Not the buzzing of panic, a thousand wasps hovering inches from your bare skin, waiting to sting.

The views are there for Brick and his stunt, anyway, not her. She'd just been lucky enough to post the clip first. An online news site had linked to her channel in an article about Brick's stream. WhomegaLil had apparently live-reacted to the clip. Teresa can see the jump in viewers for each event on her analytics page.

She slides out of bed and paces, phone in hand. Now that she doesn't go outside, she gets most of her exercise from walking in circles, around and around, looping the perimeter of her bedroom.

She checks in with the chat for her streamer group, a loose coalition of streamers who call themselves the Rainbros. Everyone in the group identifies as some stripe or another of LGBTQIA+. Sparkle-kitty is a lesbian, Ozma is trans, Jolley is transmasc nonbinary, RnBw is genderqueer, Pete45 is, in his own words, "ultrafruity," and so on. Teresa/Replay usually calls herself pansexual, though privately she also has serious doubts about her own gender identity.

She's the newest member and she still sometimes feels uncertain in the group, like a bit of an impostor, but they've all been super welcoming.

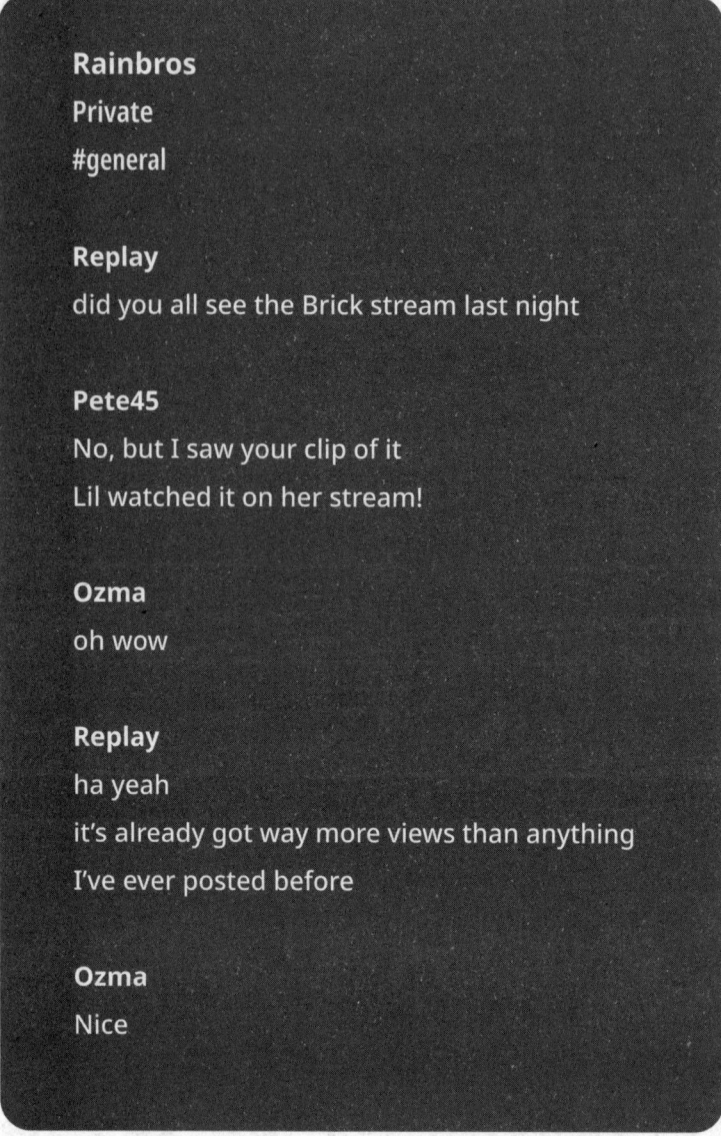

Rainbros
Private
#general

Replay
did you all see the Brick stream last night

Pete45
No, but I saw your clip of it
Lil watched it on her stream!

Ozma
oh wow

Replay
ha yeah
it's already got way more views than anything
I've ever posted before

Ozma
Nice

Pete45
New subscribers?

Replay
a few

Pete45
Well you know what sparkle would say
Make sure to cross-promote!

Replay
yeah for sure
i'll post an announcement on the clip channel
next time I go live

Ozma
Hey, I deserve partial credit for those views!
I told you to post the clip
Remember me when you get rich n famous

Replay
lol yeah don't worry
i'll save a room for you in the pool house of my
mansion

Sparklekitty and Jolley live on the West Coast, so they **probably** aren't up yet. Sparkle is the group founder and by far the most successful in terms of subscribers and views on her streams. Teresa is closest with Ozma, the only group member who lives in the same time zone. Teresa daydreams about meeting Ozma in person someday— she's only about two hours away—but she doubts it will ever really happen.

Teresa doesn't have friends in real life anymore. The few people from school who checked up on her after the accident have faded away over the past year. That's more her fault than theirs. She didn't want to see the pity in their eyes. Or the blame.

Teresa turns, starts circling her room in the other direction. She's passing by the window when a sudden needle-like pain shoots through her heel. She stifles a scream, limps over to sit on the bed, and contorts to inspect the bottom of her bare foot. At first, she can't see anything. Could it be an insect bite? A poisonous spider? Could it be here in the room? She'd notice a web, right? Did the poisonous kind even have webs? Maybe they didn't. Maybe they've infested all the dark corners. Maybe this bite will go necrotic and—

She spots it then, her neck craned over painfully, squinting. Not a bite, but a dark sliver, just under the skin.

Only a splinter. Of course. She scrapes at the sliver with a fingernail, but only succeeds in worsening the pain. It's in deep and she doesn't want to push it farther. Otherwise maybe it will never come out. It will linger there, grow infected. The infection will spread. Deepen and fester.

Teresa goes to the door. She is shaking a little now, her heart beating faster. She just needs to take the splinter out. It's fine. It's such a small thing. But a small thing can kill you.

She twists the doorknob, opens the door. Hesitates.

She's been down this hallway thousands of times. Nothing to be afraid of. Sure, there's the stairwell gaping to the left, open and exposed, but she doesn't have to go that way. She made this same walk just last night. It was fine.

Still, she runs. She knows it is only in her mind. That prickle up her spine when she turns her back to the stairwell. That feeling that something is behind her, coming up the steps.

In the bathroom, she slams the door, locks it. She has been drinking less water the last few days, so she won't have to leave her room as often.

She hasn't mentioned that to her therapist. She doesn't want to admit that her problem is getting worse, that her limits are shrinking. She should be getting better. It's been almost a year since the accident. She's supposed to be healing, moving on, living her life.

She's trying, she really is. She wants to be good. She doesn't want to be *intractable. Treatment resistant.* Sure, her therapist had used those words to describe Teresa's condition, not her as a person, but they didn't feel entirely separate. It's not like she's sick with a virus, with something you could see under a microscope. It is her own brain that's the problem. Her own thoughts.

The bathroom still feels safe, at least, even if the hallway is getting iffy.

Teresa lathers antibiotic cream on her heel, then works at the splinter with a tweezer until finally she yanks it free. Sudden relief, a minor miracle.

She hears the *thud* of a door somewhere downstairs. Probably her brother going off to school.

Teresa has been doing all her classes remotely this year. Her parents think she is spending too much time on her videos and streaming, and not enough on school, but in her opinion, only one of those has any chance of leading to a halfway-decent career.

Brick dropped out of college after his freshman year to focus on streaming. He jokes about it with his viewers, saying, "Don't follow my example, boys, this is the only thing I'm good at. One of these days you'll all get sick of me and then where will I be? Washed up, living on the streets, begging every stranger who passes by to like and subscribe. Seriously, don't be like me."

But Teresa does want to be like him. If she could trade places with Brick, trade lives, trade bodies, she'd do it in a heartbeat.

Back in her room, with the door safely shut, she pulls up the clip from Brick's stream yesterday. She opens it in her editing software, scrubs through frame by frame, isolates a couple of screenshots.

Who is the person standing behind him? Brick has a small microcosm of frequent collaborators who occasionally guest on his streams. Maybe Teresa can sleuth out the shadow figure's identity. That would be a good video for her main channel: *I Solve the Brick Mystery*. The thumbnail could be a picture of Brick with a magnifying glass superimposed, maybe her own face in the corner looking quizzical or surprised. *You'll Never Guess What I Discovered about Brick. Uncovering Brick's Biggest Mystery. This Streamer Has a DARK SECRET.*

She goes through the footage frame by frame, but can't make out a face, no matter how high she turns the brightness or the contrast. The camera just didn't pick up any features. Only the outline: human-shaped, human-sized.

She checks Brick's social media accounts. He hasn't posted

anything since last night. No explanation, no apology, not even a cryptic hint.

It *was* fake, right? He's okay?

Teresa goes further back in the footage, pinpoints the moment Brick first saw the figure—or pretended to see it—on his second monitor. He looks genuinely scared. *He's a good actor*, she thinks.

Back in middle school, Becks had convinced Teresa to try out with her for the school play once. Teresa had been terrified, but she went through with it for Becks's sake. Everything was easier when they were facing it together. The world was almost bearable.

Her mom calls up the stairs to say she's off to work. Teresa shouts down goodbye. Her dad usually works from home these days. He'll bring her up some food in a bit, if he remembers.

She should do some schoolwork, just so she can say she tried, but she's still feeling jittery from the whole splinter ordeal.

Teresa's therapist says it is important to ground herself in the physical, to stay present in the current moment, so she puts on a yoga video. She tries to follow along, doing the poses, breathing slowly in and out, but focusing on her breath is making her feel worse. Too aware. Is she breathing right? Is she getting any oxygen, really? Isn't it weird that breathing usually just happens automatically, without you even noticing, but as soon as you try to observe it, the automation stops? It becomes a thing you need to do on purpose. A task you can fail.

Teresa gives up on yoga. She sits on the floor, grabs her phone, and goes traveling.

She's at the summit of a mountain, the air thin but clear, the sky domed above in a gradient fade of pale blue to midnight, the earth's surface spread below, speckled with clouds. Majestic. Breathtaking. Teresa watches for thirty seconds, then scrolls down to the comments, the recommended videos. She clicks on another one.

Now she's under the ocean, winding through the bright corridors of a coral reef, past tiny neon fish. She watches five seconds of a video shot in Fiji. Ten seconds in Beirut. A volcano. A monsoon. A kitten in Tokyo chasing a cardboard tube.

An iceberg turns over, levering itself up out of the water like a breaching whale. The water streaming out from below is a shocking turquoise. Almost too beautiful to be real.

Teresa's phone buzzes in her hand, startling her. She pauses the video.

A notification.

Brick is live.

 Brick is live now with 13K viewers
Category: Just Chatting
OPEN THE DOOR

The lights are on again. The door is closed. Brick is sitting at his desk.

Chat

[00:02]—hi brick!
[00:03]—whoa early stream
[00:03]—YOooooo

Same place he sat the day before.

[00:05]—don't open your door bro
[00:05]—is he ok?

He is staring right into the eye of the camera.

[00:07]—brick???

Right at us.

[00:08]—HELLOO
[00:08]—earth to Brick
[00:09]—Lolwut

He seems about to say something, the briefest parting of his lips, but then he closes his mouth again.

> [00:13]—better not be any more ghosts this stream
> [00:13]—that was honestly so freaky
> [00:14]—omg I can't watch I have to go to school Nooo
> [00:14]—come on brick say something

He says nothing.

> [00:30]—chat, what is he doing
> [00:31]—this is kinda cringe ngl
> [00:31]—discomfort streamer
> [00:31]—he's meditating guys
> [00:32]—he's died

He doesn't move.

> [00:33]—omg don't say that
> [00:33]—seriously though is he okay?
> [00:34]—F
> [00:34]—F
> [00:35]—F
> [00:35]—stop it brick im scared
> [00:36]—mods???
> [00:36]—ghost got him RIP

[00:37]—whats even going on rn
[00:37]—BRICK
[00:38]—he's just on his silent arc

Brick blinks.

[00:43]—I think the stream is frozen
[00:44]—no its like that for everyone
[00:44]—r u sure?
[00:45]—earth to brick
[00:45]—why won't he move
[00:46]—!commands
[00:46]—!these are the available commands: !rules!appeal!donate!merch!mediashare!prime!sub!uptime
[00:47]—this is freaking me out
[00:47]—lol

If you watch very closely you can see he is still breathing.

3://

Teresa can't stop watching.

It shouldn't be interesting. It isn't, really.

It *is* unsettling. Creepy, even. Watching it, Teresa feels an unrelenting tension, like a held breath, waiting for something to happen.

Brick just sits there, staring at the camera in perfect silence. Nothing changes. The stream keeps going. Thirty minutes. One hour. Two. Three. Plenty of streamers have done marathon sessions, some of them staying live for days or weeks at a time, eating and sleeping on camera. But Brick isn't eating or sleeping. He isn't doing anything.

Teresa keeps the stream playing in the background as she works half-heartedly on an essay for history class. Her dad forgot to bring breakfast but arrives at her door around lunchtime, apologetic, with a sandwich. She doesn't mind. He makes a vague attempt at small talk but seems honestly relieved when she says she is busy with her schoolwork and should get back to it.

He hasn't really known how to talk to her since the accident. He treats her like a glass vase. Or a bomb. Something delicate, dangerous, best avoided if possible.

Five hours go by and Brick still hasn't moved beyond the nearly imperceptible rise and fall of his breathing. He has made no sound, has not looked away from the camera once, has not even broken eye contact except for blinking.

Why won't he move? It gives Teresa the bad kind of buzzing feeling. She turns her full attention back to the stream. With such limited stimuli, she notices things she wouldn't have otherwise. She stares at a freckle on his neck, at the hint of stubble shading along his cheeks. The tiny rectangle of the computer screen reflected in his pupils.

Now that she's stopped leaving her room, she's become an expert at noting small details in her environment. She knows the patterns of the floorboards, knows in how many places the whorls of the wood look like faces (four—two with neutral expressions, one benevolent, and one contorted in agony or rage). She knows the exact dimensions of the discolored patch in the corner of her ceiling. She stood on her bed once and measured it after becoming convinced that it was spreading, that a leak was softening the plaster bit by bit until one night the whole ceiling would fall and crush her.

She's always been a nervous person, even before the accident. *You think too much*, Becks used to say. But back then, Teresa still left her room. She left her house. She could pass as normal. If Becks noticed her zoning out, she'd flick her arm or shake her shoulder. *Get out of your head*, she'd say. There's no one to tell Teresa that, now. No one to stop her from getting entirely lost.

There is one reliable place she can turn to, though. This isn't a day Teresa usually streams, and it's still early, but she decides to make an exception.

She does her makeup, using a tiny hand mirror propped on a tissue box. She keeps messing up the eyeliner. She likes to make her eyes extra bold so they show up well on camera. The makeup feels like a disguise. A mask. It transforms her from Teresa to Replay.

She opens her broadcast software and makes a new overlay. She sets the category to "Just Chatting," titles her stream *Brickwatch—I Try to Solve the Mystery*.

She goes live.

While her waiting-to-start screen counts down, she takes a few deep breaths, then posts a link on all her social media feeds. The viewer number next to the little eye symbol ticks up. 2. 5. 17. 20. An impressive turnout! She recognizes most of the screen names. A few regulars and some fellow Brick viewers who she's been chatting with in the fan server most of the day.

She switches to her webcam. "Hey, everyone! Replay here. Welcome to a very special stream."

Sparklekitty starts every stream with "Hey there, Sparkle-kittens," and Brick usually refers to his viewers as "the boys," regardless of their actual gender variance, but Teresa isn't nearly popular enough to have a cutesy name for her viewers. It would just seem desperate.

"I suspect most of you already know, but something *super* weird is going on right now. So instead of my usual content, I am dedicating this entire stream to investigating what the hell is happening with Brick. Let's just check in on him and see what he's doing now."

She pulls in a feed of Brick's stream and sets it up to play in a smaller window beside her face. He's so motionless that it could almost be mistaken for an image rather than a video if it weren't for the constant stream of white text running down the side—his chat. Her own chat is superimposed just above.

On the laptop she's using as a second monitor, Teresa can see

her face the way it looks onstream, mirrored back to her. Her
background is her bedroom wall, the door partially visible to the
right, kind of like Brick's. The wall is blank, a flat bluish-white,
the color of a cataract. The only decoration is a set of pride flags
she color-printed at the library a few years ago. She'd like to add
more decorations, but, well, it's not like she can just pop over to
the library anymore.

"As of this moment, Brick has been live for almost six hours. So,
let's watch the entire stream from the beginning. No, really, let's do
it."

Teresa leans in close to the camera, as if she's sharing a secret
with chat. That's a mannerism she picked up from Brick, though she
didn't realize she was doing it until she watched back one of her own
VODs. "Don't panic, chat. I've sped it up a tiny bit for you."

She pulls up a two-minute time lapse she made earlier and presses
play. As she watches the first five hours of Brick's stream, sped up
and condensed, she is already thinking ahead to the end of her own
stream. She isn't sure exactly how long she'll stay live tonight, but as
soon as it is over, she'll download the VOD and edit it—along with
this timelapse and some other Brick footage—into a video for her
main channel.

She's watching the timelapse, reading chat as they react, noting the
slow climb of the viewer count, and planning the script for her video,
all of it all at once, her mind fragmenting down different paths.

This is part of what she loves about streaming: the huge pull of
mental resources required, the sheer weight of attention. It crowds
out her worries.

After she stops, of course, those worries come crashing back down on her. Or more like she's crashing down on them—as if her fear and doubt are the ground, solid and unyielding, and while she's streaming, she is keeping herself up in the air.

She stops the time lapse a minute in. Her viewer count has climbed to nearly fifty, which is unusually high for her. She's got to hook them, keep them on the line, keep them wanting more.

"Okay, so we've got the first interesting point here. Don't worry, we'll watch the rest of it in a second, but I want us all on the same page. I mean we are all on the same page already, aren't we? We're all on this same web page, you know."

She laughs, but she already regrets the pun. It's not even really a pun—just awkward enough to be bad, but not bad enough to loop back around to funny. She feels herself floundering, her energy lost.

She whips around suddenly, eyes her bedroom door. Was that a creak of the door opening? Her mother coming to talk again?

No. The door is shut. It must have been her brother down the hall or something from downstairs.

She turns back. "I thought I heard something. What do you say, chat, should I open my door?"

She is gratified to see a stream of *NO* and *omg no* and *NOoooo* racing up the chat. It's moving faster than her chat usually does.

"So today we are detectives, chat. We are going to get to the bottom of this. Together."

Weird as it sounds, even to her, she really does mean *We*, not *I*. She feels like more than just herself when she streams, feels almost like the viewers are there with her, like they are all one big organism.

"The first important question we've got to ask: *How* is Brick doing this?"

She switches back to the timelapse and lets it play as she talks through the main theories. The timelapse shows the ambient light from an unseen window tracing faintly but noticeably across Brick's back wall as the hours wear on. Time is passing, the sun is moving. This is not a looped video. She discusses the possibility that this is a prerecord or a deepfake, though she doesn't think either is likely.

"Ultimately, I favor the theory that is somehow both the simplest and the weirdest at the same time: this is real. He's really sitting there, right now, this very second. He is not moving, not taking a break to eat or drink or pee. Look, chat, it's totally possible."

She screenshares some Wikipedia entries, showing world records people have set for the longest times without eating, sleeping, and moving, all of which are longer than she would initially have guessed.

As she reads aloud, she keeps one eye, always, on that little number in the corner of her screen. It just keeps going up and up as people find their way to her stream from other sites—social media, the fan server, her video channel. It's up to seventy-five. No, eighty. Will she break a hundred?

And then the raid comes.

She and Ozma often raid each other, sending all their viewers to each other's channels. They time it so that one will start streaming as the other is about to end. Other members of their streaming friend group do it, too, a circle of support. The most popular member, Sparklekitty, raided her once. Teresa's viewership went soaring from thirty-five to six hundred in an instant. It settled back down to seventy after a while. But still, she'd kept some of them.

This is on a whole different level. There's one comment in chat: *RAID*. And then suddenly the whole chat is absolutely flooded, streaming past faster than she can read. Her viewer count goes wild.

The raid is from KingCoal. She's never talked to the guy before in her life, but she's watched his streams. He's a friend of Brick's and has almost as many subscribers. Teresa can hardly believe it.

Is this it? The moment everything changes for her? Her parents want her to leave her room, go to college, live a normal life. But she isn't sure she can do that. What if she could just stream for the rest of her life? Make a living at it. Become a professional, like Brick, like KingCoal.

She's getting ahead of herself. It's too soon to know. All she knows for certain is that number in the corner. Almost five thousand! An unfathomable number.

So many people, so many eyes. She's got them in this moment. Now she needs to keep them. She needs to stay up in the air for as long as she can. She can't fall.

↑
3768

r/LivestreamFail · Posted by user/enjolradical 2 hours ago

↓

Brick does literally nothing

https://clips.tv/:DoubtfulTolerantSpiderPlanking-YKdWhp4WXI9j8fQR

291 comments

Memesaur3 · 2 hours ago

Mans is onto something. Go hard, get big, give up.

↑ 987 ↓ Reply Share Report Save

> **bettasplenda** · 2 hours ago
>
> at this point dude could probably stream himself sitting on the toilet taking a shit and 50k people would tune in
>
> ↑ 431 ↓ Reply Share Report Save

> > **s@uroncylon** · 1 hour ago
> >
> > I'm honestly surprised he hasn't done that yet
> >
> > ↑ 220 ↓ Reply Share Report Save

whichthat · 2 hours ago

And yet he still has 1,0000000000x as many viewers as me (╯°□°)╯︵ ┻━┻

↑ 608 ↓ Reply Share Report Save

wrdfilu · 1 hour ago

bruh can someone explain what is going on in this clip

↑ 524 ↓ Reply Share Report Save

> **brick_poggers** · 1 hour ago
>
> ¯_(ツ)_/¯
>
> ↑ 176 ↓ Reply Share Report Save

pitomba999 · 1 hour ago

Am I the only one who remembers when the successful streamers were the ones who were actually good at games?

↑ 294 ↓ Reply Share Report Save

> **toitle_p0wer** · 1 hour ago
>
> yes you are
>
> ↑ 1.1K ↓ Reply Share Report Save

Rainbros
Private
#general

Replay
omfg
kingocal just raided
*kingcoal
im live rn

RnBw
holy shit
seriously?

Jolley
WHAT?

Sparklekitty
Congrats!!

Ozma
Ah I'm still at work!!
Post a clip later pls
How many viewers?

Replay
so many
im freaking out

RnBw

jealous

but u deserve it!

Sparklekitty

Make the most of it

Give them an incentive to subscribe

This is a huge opportunity

How long are you going to stream?

Make sure to raid one of us when you're done

4://

Her therapist has never come right out and said he thinks Teresa shouldn't stream, but he's implied as much. A judgmental tilt of the head when the subject comes up. Questions that imply an answer. *Isn't it dangerous, to be so visible online?*

If it is, Teresa doesn't care. Right now, she's flying. The pulse of chat messages up the left side of the screen is keeping pace with her mind for once, fueling her. She is high on it. This is the best she has felt in months, the most alive, the most real.

She's been asking viewers to share their theories, running polls in the chat. She feels almost like a conductor in front of an orchestra.

The most popular theory according to the polls: that Brick's streams are part of an ARG—an augmented reality game—planned for the viewers to pick apart like a puzzle. He wouldn't be the first streamer to run one. The second-most popular theory is a psychotic break. The third is something supernatural.

Teresa dissects Brick's stream from the day before, going through the moment the shadowy figure arrived frame by frame. It looks translucent in some shots, which supports the idea that the figure is digital trickery, rather than a person in a mask.

Next, she looks up the viewer who donated the suggestion to "open the door" in the first place, to see if that part was staged. It could very well be a fake account. No followers, no profile picture. The username Tjbnfskha is a generic keysmash.

Teresa has some fun trying out different potential pronunciations, in case Brick meant the name as a clue. Her chat says to run it through an anagram generator, which turns up the words *thanks, ankhs, banks, baths, hanks, shaft*, and her personal favorite, *stank*, as possibilities. But there's no perfect match. The name seems genuinely meaningless.

Teresa likes unpicking mysteries, doing deep-dive research. It's the same way she copes with things that scare her, by learning as much as humanly possible about them. How many hours has she spent reading about rabies, blood clots, prions, and environmental collapse? Hundreds, probably. She could earn an honorary doctorate in fear.

She uses another website to look up which channels Tjbnfskha follows. If it was only Brick, this would be a dead giveaway that it was Brick's secret alt account, but there's a follow list of ten.

> Brick
> WhomegaLil
> KingCoal
> hedgelord
> horsegirl4
> 6bluemarbles
> important_pigeon
> GameGammaRay
> Lie25
> paracheirodon

Teresa goes through them one by one. The first five are all big names, but the ones after that are people Teresa's never heard of. She reminds chat not to harass any of these smaller streamers. There's no proof that any of them are involved.

The ninth one down—Lie25—seems to have stopped streaming, their page devoid of any activity. Teresa tries googling the name. The top result is a news article from a small-town paper.

She reads the first line. "Twenty-three-year-old local resident Kyle Schaeffer died Saturday evening while engaged in the popular online activity of livestreaming himself playing video games," which is clearly a sentence written by someone Extremely Old. Still, it gives Teresa a sick feeling. She's surprised she hasn't heard of the guy before, if he really did die while streaming. Then again, at any given hour of the day, there are thousands of people streaming on this one platform alone.

Teresa clicks away from the page. Her chat is suggesting the article could be fake—part of the ARG—but Teresa shuts them down. They need to assume this is a real person who really died. They need to be respectful.

She decides to abandon the thread of the follow list. She tells chat it's because she doesn't think it's connected to the central mystery, but the truth is that the article scared her.

A real person who really died.

She's got to be careful, with this many viewers. Already the chat is more unruly than usual. She's had to ban several people for using slurs. Sparklekitty and all the bigger streamers use volunteers to moderate their chat for them, but Teresa has never needed to before. In the group chat, she asks for advice and RnBw and Jolley both offer to come help moderate.

Sometimes streaming feels like a collaborative and supportive space. Sometimes it feels more like a mad race with everyone scrambling over one another, pointing wildly at whoever is winning and shouting "I know them!" while chat waits at the bottom, a seething mass of hungry eyes egging streamers on, hoping they'll do something wild.

But Teresa loves streaming, despite the occasional downsides. It saved her life.

She couldn't do much in the first few weeks after the accident, with a broken collarbone and multiple fractures, but she desperately needed a distraction from the pain and from her own thoughts. Her memories. Becks smiling. Becks sitting beside her in the car. Becks, who was gone now forever.

So she'd watch videos. Cats, cringe, compilations. A constant drip. At some point, the algorithm fed her a clip of Brick. Just a short one of him laughing so hard he fell out of his computer chair. It made her smile. Which was rare in those early days. Kind of a big deal. She binged all his videos, started tuning in for his streams. She thought Becks would have liked him, too. Wished she could show her.

The first time Teresa ever streamed herself, it was on a whim, about two months after the accident. Her collarbone was mostly healed, but she was having panic attacks every time she left the house.

She streamed for thirty-five minutes. Zero viewers, but somehow the mere act of streaming made her feel less alone. Talking out loud to herself, pretending that someone *might* be watching—it took her mind away from everything. A relief. A brief respite.

The second time she streamed, she found a ripped version of a vintage game she and Becks had played at the library when they were kids, a clunky park simulator so old she had to install an extra program to even get her computer to recognize it.

She streamed for an hour and fifteen minutes. Around halfway through, her view count popped from zero to one. The singular viewer stayed for about five minutes and then left.

Maybe that should have been discouraging, but Teresa wasn't bothered. In fact, she found it exhilarating. She had been a part of that person's day, even if only for a little while.

So she kept it up, stream after stream, slowly figuring out what worked and what didn't.

On her stream now, Teresa is going through clips from Brick's old streams to see if any of them might hold clues. Ozma and Jolley both call in to keep her company and help keep the energy up. They banter a bit, compare theories.

Teresa and Jolley have talked on the phone a few times before, though not nearly as often as she and Ozma. Mostly, they've just discussed streaming logistics, but their talks occasionally strayed over into personal shit—school, favorite bands, gender identity. Jolley came out as nonbinary when they were only twelve, which honestly makes Teresa kind of jealous.

Teresa has thought about using *they*, has tried the word on like a coat. The *she* coat doesn't quite fit, but she's used to it. She can hide inside it. *They* feels like a flashy coat, one with sequins, maybe, or bold stripes. Something that will call attention to its wearer, and Teresa isn't sure she's ready for that.

Still, she sometimes thinks of her online persona, Replay, as entirely genderless, the way she'd like to be.

She keeps streaming longer than she intended to, longer than she ever has before. Her stream slowly bleeds viewers as the night wears on. She tries not to focus on that little number going down, tries not to feel it as a loss, as something almost physically depleting.

She thinks she might keep streaming all night. As long as Brick stays live, so will she. She switches to a game for a while, though she keeps his stream's feed playing in the left corner. Her own camera is turned off, so any new viewers just tuning in might be confused for a second, might think he is the one playing the game.

On Brick's stream, the room darkens around him. His eyes, perhaps, are getting more bloodshot. Nothing else changes.

Until 1:16 a.m.

Teresa is playing a cooperative ghost-hunting game, cleaning up digital hauntings with Jolley and Sparklekitty. Ozma was playing with them for a while but had to log off. Teresa is sorry to miss out on their usual evening phone call, but Ozma assured her via private message that they could catch up tomorrow.

In the game, Teresa's jerky avatar is roaming the halls of a basic suburban house, not so different from her own, though the rooms here are subsumed by a hazy fog. She ascends the stairs, runs the thready beam of her flashlight over the landing. It flickers on and off, illuminates one closed door and one open doorway leading to a bathroom, the clawfoot tub like a hunched beast in the shadows.

"Nothing down here," says Sparkle on their group call.

"Did either of you check the bedroom?" Teresa asks.

Down in the left corner of the screen, Brick jerks in his chair. A slight convulsive jolt. It's the most he's moved in hours.

"Did you see that?" Teresa asks.

"See what?" asks Jolley, who is just playing the game.

"Hold on," Teresa says. "Brick just did something. I'll be right back."

She pauses the game, minimizes it, and makes Brick's feed full screen again. Her chat is freaking out. They all saw it too, of course. She mutes the call, addresses them directly, breathless.

"What the hell was that, chat?"

She turns her own camera back on, tries not to worry that her makeup has smudged around her left eye. She is Replay, now. Painful self-consciousness is Teresa's thing.

"Did he nearly fall asleep or something? I'll have to clip that so we can watch it back."

She doesn't do that just yet, though. Doesn't do anything. She's watching, waiting to see if he'll move again. She can almost feel everyone else on her stream, all her viewers craning toward their screens, waiting along with her.

Brick gasps.

An odd sudden intake of breath. The first noise he has made all stream. It's not a nice noise. Phlegmy, asthmatic.

"Is he okay?" Without really meaning to, Teresa has leaned so far forward in her chair that her face is mere inches away from her screen, inches away from Brick's own face.

And then he speaks.

His first word comes out halting, rusty, like the creaking of a door hinge.

Was it even a word? It sounded like "I" but maybe it was just a noise. Teresa isn't sure.

She doesn't have to wonder for long because Brick repeats himself a moment later.

"I am . . ." he says more clearly, though still in a strange tone of voice. He seems to be moving his mouth as little as possible, the words barely squeezing out, air forced through a narrow gap.

He takes a breath, speaks again.

"I am scared."

Brick FINALLY BREAKS his silence!!

16,479 views . . . SHARE   DOWNLOAD   CLIP   SAVE

 ReplayClips   SUBSCRIBE

2.5k subscribers

witchfever 1 hour ago

Whoa this literally JUST happened on his stream how is this channel so fast?

> **addddddddddddddy** 1 hour ago
>
> Check out my channel it is way better

GhostedTrashCat 30 minutes ago

I am scared also

blu3b3rryb4g3l 28 minutes ago

I genuinely think someone needs to check on him this gave me goose bumps I don't think he is well

Takemetoforks224 25 minutes ago

He is faking for attention

Brick speaks AGAIN

9,876 views . . . SHARE   DOWNLOAD   CLIP   SAVE

 ReplayClips   SUBSCRIBE
2.5k subscribers

hailey_004 15 minutes ago (edited)
okay now this is some straight-up horror movie shit

> **11235813** 5 minutes ago
> Finally its here wtch.tv/?%v=neVeRJHP9wJ

> **s012** 5 minutes ago
> It is finally here wtch.tv/%?v=9g0nNa8j&LK

> **mycatcalledluna.** 3 minutes ago
> why so many bots

CiCi0430 4 minutes ago
Do not tell me this man just said "look behind you"?! 😬

> **waternymph99** 3 minutes ago
> we all watched the same video you don't have to repeat it

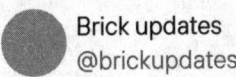

Brick updates
@brickupdates

He spoke a third time!!
"Is this real?"—Brick

25 Reposts 10 Quotes 900 Likes

Raphael R. (they/them) @glassarmonica
replying to @brickupdates

he's the voice of a generation lol

Chelsea Is Reading @bookswithchelsea
replying to @brickupdates

**I need to go to bed but I can't now this
is killing me**

Sophie @fizzy.sophie1023
replying to @brickupdates

ARG pog

 Replay is live now with 343 viewers
Category: Just Chatting
I SOLVE THE BRICK MYSTERY

Replay, a teenager in an oversized black hoodie, sits in a desk chair in front of a mostly blank wall. Her winged eyeliner is smudged at the corners, wings clipped. Her brown hair is back in a loose pony-tail but some of the strands have escaped.

> **Chat**
>
> [3:23:07]—my mom says I gotta go to bed bye chat!

She looks tired.

> [3:23:09]—you look tired

But not as tired as Brick, who takes up more of the screen than she does.

> "I don't know. Like, everything he has said so far is trending. So it could be deliberate. Like viral marketing, you know?"

> [3:23:13]—what is he sellin tho

Replay clicks something. The feed of Brick's stream is replaced by a

Google Doc where she's keeping track of everything he's said so far.

> I am scared
> Look behind you
> Is this real
> The door is open
> Do it

[3:23:22]—maybe it is song lyrics
[3:23:23]—ugh NOT another streamer trying to have a music career

"I mean, that last one is like one word off a corporate slogan, anyway."

She looks at the camera.

"Don't forget, chat, consumerism is killing us all.
On an unrelated note, buy my merch."

She grins, then sort of flinches, like she's embarrassed by herself.

[3:23:34]—go back to the brick stream

"That's a joke. I don't have merch. And I'm not trying to shit-talk anybody who does. I mean . . ."

She lunges out of frame for a moment, returns holding up a beanie with an embroidered rainbow-colored cat.

[3:23:41]—lol I have that same hat

"See! Go sub to Sparklekitty, by the way."

[3:23:46]—switch back pls

"Calm down, chat. I've got a timer going. The pattern has held so far. If you're just joining my stream, by the way, welcome!

"But yes, there does seem to be a pattern. He speaks ten to thirteen minutes apart each time, so we've still got at least a minute."

[3:24:02]—switch back he might talk again!

"Okay, fine, chat, hold your horses."

She switches away from the Google Doc, back to the feed of Brick.

[3:24:07]—thank u

Replay sits in silence for a while, mirroring Brick. Watching, waiting.

She says, "I guess—"

Brick speaks again.

Replay slaps a hand over her mouth.

> [3:24:42]—AHHHH
> [3:24:43]—he spoke!

"Oh dang, that was early. I'm sorry, chat. I'll get a clip of it. What did he say? Something about commands?"

> [3:24:50]—These are the available commands
> [3:24:51]—so random

"'These are the available commands'? Huh. That's the weirdest one yet.

"The others fit together better, I think. Like they could almost be a sentence, or a call and response. And some of them are clearly referencing yesterday's stream. 'Open the door.' 'Look behind you.'"

> [3:25:09]—no wait I've seen that before

[3:25:09]—look

"This sounds like a game menu. Maybe that's the plot of the ARG—Brick has been sucked into a game? And like we're the players and he's the NPC? That could be cool."

She's reading chat on her other monitor.

[3:25:20]—!commands
[3:25:20]—these are the available commands: !rules!appeal!donate! merch!mediashare!prime!sub!uptime

"Oh, huh."

She switches the screen to her own feed, so now she's in the corner of the screen and then she's also behind herself, smaller, and behind herself again even smaller, and so on, repeating in a line down to some invisible infinity.

Chat is repeated too. She scrolls the feed backward a few seconds. It's out of sync now, the Replays behind the real one all from slightly in the past.

She freeze-frames, zooms into the chat log.

[3:23:51]—look

```
[3:23:53]—!commands
[3:23:53]—these are the available commands:
!rules!appeal!donate!merch!mediashare!prime!
sub!uptime
[3:25:32]—Lol it is us
[3:25:33]—We r so famous
```

"So it's just an auto-programmed chat command?
Why is he saying that?"

She switches back to the list of everything he's said so far.

> [3:25:39]—maybe it's a coincidence
> [3:25:39]—I guess Brick is chat now
> [3:25:40]—one of us! one of us!
> [3:25:40]—he's become chat lol
> [3:25:41]—how the turns have tabled

She frowns, reads chat again.

"He is chat? He's become chat? You guys are self-obsessed, aren't you? Although . . ."

> [3:25:50]—streamers are the self-obsessed ones

She pulls up her own video channel. Plays back the clip she'd posted the day before, of the shadowy figure appearing on Brick's stream.

She pauses it, points to the side, the little rectangle of Brick's chat.

"Yeah, someone did type 'look behind you' right
after the figure showed up."

[3:26:05]—he is plagiarizing lol
[3:26:06]—whoa

She lets the clip play out a little longer, then pauses again, straightens up in her chair, sounding excited.

"And there's 'the door is open' and 'I am scared.'
See, in all caps right there. He's just repeating
random things from chat. We cracked it!"

[3:26:48]—omg yeah someone says
DO IT during the water bottle bit

She's leaning forward, her eyes bright again, more awake.

"This is great. So, what's up, is he reading it? Or
are those pre-scripted phrases and he had col-
laborator accounts type them out in chat, know-
ing he'd repeat them later? Like foreshadowing?"

[3:26:53]—Look behind you

"Look behind me? Ha, yeah right, nice one, chat.

I'm not falling for that."

Behind her, in her room, the bedroom door is creaking open.

[3:27:01]—behind you replay

Brick's door was painted flat white. A modern house. A modern door.

Her house is older. The door is made from darkly stained wood. There are scratches and grooves worn into the panels.

[3:27:05]—open the door

The knob is a heavily patinaed brass, carved with a sunburst of fili-gree. They don't bother with door handles like that anymore. Just featureless chrome-plated orbs.

[3:27:07]—no seriously look behind you

Regardless, Replay's door is opening. Slow, painfully slow. The hall-way beyond it is dark.

[3:27:09]—Replay behind you!!

"Stop it, chat, it's not that funny."

[3:27:14]—we aren't joking
[3:27:15]—yeah ur door is open

She turns her gaze off to the side, where she can see what her stream looks like. The door has swung open nearly all the way.

Replay jumps up from her chair, twisting around to face the door, arms up, defensive. She is breathing hard. You can see her sides heaving.

[3:27:20]—is this for real?
[3:27:21]—Replay?
[3:27:21]—wait is she part of the ARG

There is a shadow beyond the door. A shape. A figure, standing in the hallway.

[3:27:28]—oh my god not this again

"What the *fuck*. There is nothing there. There is nothing. I swear. The door is closed. This is like. It's just like—"

[3:27:35]—it's a trick right?
[3:27:36]—it has to be
[3:27:36]—this can't be real

The figure has grown clearer. It's not just a shadow. It's a person. A man. Though we can't see his face.

The light from the room should be falling on him, illuminating his features, but it isn't, somehow.

He steps forward into the room.

[3:27:42]—No!

5://

Teresa slams her laptop shut. So hard it bounces on the desk. She drops to her knees, grabs the power strip cord, and yanks it out of the wall.

She is shaking. Time has slowed to a thick, sticky syrup.

As she stands, she sees her own stricken reflection in the black screen of her dead monitor. The house is quiet. She whips around to look at her door. It is closed.

It has always been closed.

Her heart is going so fast she begins to shiver. As if she is cold. But she doesn't feel cold. Her insides are just trying to shake their way out of her skin, trying to run off to safety. Her teeth chatter. A horrible clacking. Bone on bone. Her skull rattling.

She tries to slow her breathing, she really does. She remembers her therapist once suggested she try plunging her face in cold water when she's panicking. It apparently triggers a reflex that slows your pulse. Presumably as a last-ditch effort to help you survive when you're about to drown in a frozen lake.

Which isn't a comforting thought.

She'd still try it, though. Her heart is going so fast it is almost painful. Except there's no way she can walk down the hallway to the bathroom now.

She stares hard at the door, as if daring it to move.

It was exactly like Brick described on his stream yesterday. She could clearly see the door opening on her laptop feed. She could see the figure. That person where no person should be. Standing in her doorway. Moving toward her. A single, almost hesitant step.

But she could only see that on the stream. When she turned around, her door was closed. When she turned around, she was alone.

Had Brick been telling the truth? How could that be?

She tries to approach the door, but her fear is an invisible wall. The air feels too dense. She can't breathe.

This is a panic attack. It is just a panic attack. The air is normal and her heart is fast, yes, a terrified, trapped animal, but it won't kill her. It can't kill her there is no one there the door is closed it has always been closed she is alone.

She moves forward, step by painful step. It is only her room. Her room is safe. There is no one here. No one no one no one.

By the time she reaches the door, by the time she curls her hand around the doorknob, she is breathing in short, sharp bursts. She can hear her own blood rushing, feel every *thump* of her heart like a punch to the sternum. She should turn the knob, open the door. Look out. Reassure herself there is nothing but an empty hallway.

She cannot.

"Fuck," she says aloud. This is ridiculous. But the door looks like a threat now. It has been reclassified in her mind and there's nothing she can do. It's gone the same way as the stairs, the first floor, the backyard, the street, the rest of the world: it isn't safe anymore.

She stares at the door, her unease growing. She'd give anything for a lock. A nice big dead bolt, maybe.

As quietly as she can, she pulls the drawers from her dresser, then pushes the empty body of it over to block the door. She puts all the drawers back in, considers. She can still see the top of the door, can still imagine it creaking open. It's not enough.

She moves her bed, too, nudges the frame over inch by inch. Then she levers the mattress up, hefting its awkward bulk onto one side and letting it fall against the dresser at an angle.

Now she can't see the door at all.

The effort has calmed her, slightly. Or at least given purpose to her adrenaline. She hopes the sound didn't wake anyone in the house. It is late, very late.

She'd really like to text Ozma, but she's almost definitely asleep by now and she needs to get up early for work. Teresa doesn't want to risk waking her and ruining her whole shift. Jolley, though, is all the way on the West Coast, in an earlier time zone. She texts them.

hey, did you happen to be watching the end of my stream?

Jolley
No, sorry

Why?

Did something happen?

oh no, it was nothing

nevermind

She realizes she doesn't want to say it. Saying it would make it too real. Maybe it really was nothing. Could she have imagined the figure? Hallucinated it? She thinks she read once that something like 95 percent of supernatural phenomena could easily be explained by simple sleep deprivation. She hasn't slept well the last few nights. Hasn't slept well in a long time, honestly.

Chat saw it too, though, didn't they? They told her to look behind her.

Maybe *that's* what made her see it. The power of suggestion. Maybe they were just trolling.

She tells herself that and she halfway believes it, but not enough to turn her computer back on. Not enough to dismantle the furniture barricade.

Instead, she pulls the sheets and the comforter off her bed and piles them in the farthest corner from the door. She settles down into the pile like a burrowing animal, drawing the comforter over her head.

She sits there for a long time, back pressed hard into the angle of the wall, watching the door. Listening to the ticking of her own heartbeat in her ears.

When she falls, finally, it is into a restless sleep, broken often by bad dreams. Several times, she bolts awake in a nameless panic.

After the first time, she gropes for her phone. It has switched itself into nighttime mode. Past a certain hour, the screen grays itself out and hides all notifications. Her mother insisted she set that up. It's supposed to keep her from spending all night on her phone.

It doesn't, of course. Though it does lend a sort of dreamish, old-movie quality to anything she looks at late. She puts on a video, *Twelve Hours of Ambient Jellyfish to Study or Relax To*. She sets the phone back on the floor, pointed up, so it casts a muted underwater light around the room.

By the morning, she has convinced herself that nothing happened last night. Chat was just messing with her, trying to get a rise out of a streamer. They succeeded. She was suggestible. She'd been playing that clip of Brick's door opening over and over, after all, squinting at the shadowy figure behind him. So it's no wonder her brain provided similar imagery.

She reaches for her phone. It's back in color now and notifications flood the screen. More than usual. New emails, new texts, new snaps, new DMs.

All about the same thing. Last night's stream.

One message from Ozma has a link to a video clip.

Teresa doesn't want to watch it. With the gentle morning sun pouring softly through her window, it is easier to believe that everything is fine. That it was just her anxiety. That the world is safe.

Her therapist would be so proud. Her therapist would tell her to put the phone down, to walk away.

She clicks the link.

Small-Time Streamer Stalked By GHOST

3,876 views . . . SHARE   DOWNLOAD   CLIP   SAVE

StreamHighlights   SUBSCRIBE
10k subscribers

Milk.Toast 15 minutes ago (edited)
Who the hell is she? Is she working with Brick?

> **Js_269** 5 minutes ago
> Brick secret channel wtch.tv?v=G1vE2C#IBFI1

Bourneroyalty 4 minutes ago
Wow she looks like a mess

> **ayeayefitlike** 4 minutes ago
> mid

itskharina 3 minutes ago
this is well done honestly

pizza_goblin 3 minutes ago
She legal? Or am I going to jail lmao

Sparklekitty

That was wild!

You should have warned us you were

planning something like that

How did you do it?

You'd tell us if you were doing a secret

collab with Brick, right?

Replay?

Well congrats lol you are trending

sorry

i fell asleep

Ha it's okay girl

I don't know how you pulled that off

It looked so real like omg scary 😭

Are you going to stream again today?

You definitely should

We could coordinate raids

i'm not sure

i'm pretty tired

Omg you have to

You've got so much buzz right now

I'm planning a group party game

stream on my channel later

You can join us

sure

you should go live on your channel
for a bit first
and then raid

okay

Ozma
hey I was asleep when you ended the stream
Sparkle sent me a link
you made it to one of the bigger clip channels!
wtch.tv/?%y=Yo0u453jCh6
you okay?
text me when you're up or I'll worry my
whole shift

sorry!
just saw this

it's totally fine.
work is slow this morning anyway

no endless stream of soccer moms
demanding caramel macchiatos?

ha no they all have white wine hangovers I
guess

but seriously
are you okay?
were you just pretending with all that?

                                        no

no you aren't okay or no you
weren't pretending

                              ugh, both
                    i wasn't pretending
              ozma I have no idea what's going

Oh damn

                        am I losing my mind???

minds are overrated
Do you want me to call when I get off work?

                        yeah that would be great
                            this is all so weird
              sparkle wants me to stream with her later

That's cool
Do you want to?

                                    i don't know

she's being kind of insistent about it

That's just how she is
She knows this business
That clip of you is getting a ton of views

yeah
my DMs are FULL right now
a million strangers trying to talk to me
its kinda overwhelming

ok sudden rush here
I gotta go but I'll call as soon I can
hangintherecat.gif

← **Message requests** • • •

Rosemary Fields @rosemaryfields   10m
Was that real? If it was then . . .

Kryara @kryara   15m
Hey I was wondering if you would . . .

Lemons @Libra_loves_lemons_a_lot   20m
Please check out my channel and . . .

Jasmine @jasm1ne4may0r   30m
Sent you a link

John C. @gibbety   1hr
Hey u single babygirl I want to . . .

Geoff with a G @geoffoff   1hr
Sent you a photo

Kayleigh @kle674gurl   1hr
Fuck off from brick you fucking . . .

Bademandme @bademandme   2hr
Are you possessed by a demon?

Pibble the Cat @PibbletheCat   2hr
Let's collab

Beth @_beth_bby_   2hr
R u working with Brick?

Meg Smit @megagorgon   3hr
Kill urself

6://

Her therapist said stay off the internet. Her therapist said solve a crossword, read a book, reorganize your sock drawer. Teresa's got a crossword website open in one tab. An e-book open in another. She watched two whole minutes of a laundry-folding ASMR video.

She's trying.

But it takes more and more to fill up the empty space sometimes, to keep her own thoughts from rushing in. She has to keep up the constant drip, has to pour more and more into herself—a new piece of art, a new atrocity, a new celebrity couple, a new song, a new remix of the new song, a new joke, a new murder, a new meme, a new perversion of the new meme by a corporate brand account, a new politician doing something despicable, a new beach body to be jealous of, a new baby panda just born, a new species of beetle gone forever from this earth before she'd ever even heard of it. It was green, with a slight shimmer to its wings. About the size of a fingernail.

Even when it is relentless and terrible, all this input, it's still better than the alternative. Better than silence, stillness, space. Better than giving her own thoughts room to rush in.

They have been waiting all this time, just off to one side, and they are ready.

Remember, they say. They demand it. Pulling back the eyelids of her mind, so she can't look away. *Remember that night in the car.*

Remember just one second of it, over and over. Your whole life con-
densed to a bright, hot point of fear and pain. Remember a strand
of hair, wet and dark. Remember the trees and the pavement and the
blackboard sky. Remember that you are going to die.

You are going to die.

There is no other way out of this place. No other door.

Someone knocks on Teresa's bedroom door, now.

"Sweetie," her mom calls, "are you awake?" She jiggles the door
handle, trying to open the door, the sound muffled slightly by the
mattress. "Honey?" Her voice is getting higher, which means she's
worried. "Open up, please."

"I can't," says Teresa, but her mom must not hear her, because
she keeps shouting.

"Teresa. Open this door right now!" She's full-on shrill now. The
door bangs against the dresser as she tries to push it open, but the
blockade holds.

Teresa shouts back. "I can't."

"What's happening? Are you hurt? Do I need to call 911?"

Calm down, Teresa wants to tell her, though she realizes this is
hypocritical.

"No, Mom," she says, getting as close to the door as she dares.
She doesn't know how to explain it. "I just can't open the door right
now. I'm sorry."

"What is this? What's blocking the door?" The mattress shakes as
her mother tries the door again and again.

"It's just the dresser. Please don't try to force it."

"I have your breakfast, Teresa. You need to open the door."

"I'm not hungry right now. But I'm fine, I swear."

"I'm getting your father."

Her mother's footsteps recede. Teresa sighs, retreats to the opposite side of the room again. She checks her phone. More message requests have poured in since last time she checked it, about ten minutes ago. Some of them are fine. But a lot of them aren't.

Some people are accusing her of copying Brick. Some have decided that his weird behavior must be her fault. Some seem simply to be mad that she's a girl. Like how dare she.

She shouldn't keep reading the bad ones. But it feels unsafe to leave them lurking in there, unknown dangers.

She finds four veiled death threats, three overt ones, about a dozen messages that are sexually explicit, three that mention doxxing, and one that describes what the user plans to do to her in such violent detail that she finally stops reading.

She posts: *To everyone asking after last night's stream, yes I'm okay and no I'm not working with Brick,* and then she deletes it less than a minute later because it's a lie.

She is absolutely not okay.

Her subscriber count has gone up on all her channels, though. In addition to the Brick clips, she posted a clip from her own stream of the moment the shadowy figure appeared. She hated to do it, but it seemed only fair she should get some of the views herself.

It still scares her fresh, every time she sees the footage. Her own face. Her own room. The door creaking open.

It makes no sense. How had that thing appeared on her stream? In real life, when she'd physically turned around, she'd seen nothing. And yet it was clearly there on the screen, and in the recording when she was watched it back this morning.

Before, Teresa thought Brick was probably playing a game, putting on a show, but now she's sure he isn't. The shadowy figure appearing on his stream was real. Which means his current catatonia must be real, too.

Is the same thing going to happen to her?

Her dad knocks. She can tell it's him because his knocking is so hesitant. Like a little bird pecking at a seed. "Teresa?" he says. His voice is hesitant, too. "Are you in *crisis* right now?"

Teresa rolls her eyes. That must be the word her mother used when she told him to come up here. A scrap of lingo she's picked up from Teresa's therapist.

Her dad wouldn't have come on his own. His way of dealing with Teresa's "problem" was mostly to pretend that there wasn't one. She honestly prefers that approach to her mother's anxious hovering. At least he leaves her alone most of the time.

"No," she says. "I'm fine. Everything's fine."

"So, um, can you open the door?"

Sometimes she thinks her father is a little afraid of her. Or maybe not her, precisely, but what she represents. A threat. To normality. To his fantasy of a happy model family.

"I had a rough night," she says. "I just really need a little space to myself, so I can process some emotions." She's laying it on thick, throwing the lingo right back, using the words she thinks will appease. "I've got to heal at my own pace, you know? So please respect my boundaries about this."

"Okay," says her father. "Sure. I'll just leave your bagel here outside the door. Let us know if you want to talk."

Her dad will go down and tell her mom not to worry so much and probably the two of them will have a fight about it. But that doesn't feel like her problem right now.

Her problem right now is Brick.

She wishes she could get in touch with someone who actually knows him, but he's so many leagues of success above her that their circles barely overlap. The closest she can get to a connection is Sparklekitty, who played a few rounds of that social deduction space game with WhomegaLil the year before.

Sparkle is great at networking. She seems fearless about contacting people. Brick is like that too. He's always inviting different streamers to play "You Laugh You Lose" with him, or to appear as guests on the monthly variety show he hosts on his stream.

Fearlessness is not a quality Teresa shares. Still, her fear of whatever is happening right now is stronger than her fear of social faux pas. She sends Sparkle a message asking her if she can get in touch with WhomegaLil. She tries to message Lil directly, too, but of course Lil is probably deluged with messages all the time.

Brick has mentioned onstream before that he lives in San Antonio. For his first year of streaming, he was still living in his parent's house, but he's got his own apartment now. It's near a bar—he complains sometimes about the music bleeding into his streams.

Does she know anyone from Texas? She thinks maybe Pete mentioned something about a cousin in Austin once. She sends him a message, then pulls up some VODs of Brick's old streams, looking for anything that might help. KingCoal flew out to visit him all the way from England once. They did a cooking stream together in Brick's kitchen. You get a quick glimpse out the kitchen window at one point, though there isn't much to see. Just a high slatted fence.

Half an hour later, Teresa is trawling through Street View on Google Maps, clicking her way down streets near bars in San Antonio, looking for wooden fences in the right shade of brown.

It's ridiculous. She knows it is ridiculous, but she's got to do something. Or at least *feel* like she's doing something. When she spots a likely fence, she searches the address, tries to find any old sale or rent listings with pictures of the inside.

There. That one. The counter is the same. And the layout of one of the upstairs bedrooms.

Could this be Brick's address?

Maybe Pete's cousin from Austin would drive down and check. Pete hasn't gotten back to her yet. She feels helpless. She checks all her various social media accounts, skimming over the flood of messages. She's finally stopped reading every single one.

But here's a notification she was waiting for. Earlier in the day, she'd made several comments on an old post about Kyle/Lie25, hoping to get more information. Someone has replied.

She isn't sure if this guy Kyle's death is connected to what's happening now. She hopes it isn't. But she needs to know.

r/Livestreaming · Posted by user/ilovemydogsprinkles 46 days ago

↑

57

↓

Streamer dies onstream??

Has anybody heard of this guy Lie25? I found an article saying he died while

streaming. How did he die? Was it actually ON the stream? Like is there video

or something?

ETA link to article: https://url.c@m/uP7fc7e3UP

9 comments

Malorei · 46 days ago

Wow I'd never heard of him either. Seems like a big deal if true.

First onstream death?

↑ **17** ↓ Reply Share Report Save

> **Inmywildestdreams13** · 46 days ago
>
> Nah he's not the first. Weren't there two players that died during
>
> some livestreamed tournament in hong kong or something? Like just
>
> chugged energy drinks for twenty-four hours and had heart attacks.
>
> ↑ **5** ↓ Reply Share Report Save

Big_julio568739 · 46 days ago

It was an overdose

↑ **12** ↓ Reply Share Report Save

> **thecloudslooklikeyou** · 46 days ago
>
> how do you know that?
>
> ↑ **2** ↓ Reply Share Report Save

Big_julio568739 · 45 days ago

I live like one town over, people talk

↑ 7 ↓ Reply Share Report Save

Replayyy · 1 hour ago

Hey I don't know if you'll see this, but would you be willing to answer some questions? I'm trying to find more information about this.

↑ 0 ↓ Reply Share Report Save

LaceratedGrapes · 44 days ago

There's video. I've seen it.

↑ 8 ↓ Reply Share Report Save

ilovemydogsprinkles OP · 44 days ago

Link?

↑ 2 ↓ Reply Share Report Save

LaceratedGrapes · 43 days ago

I'll dm it to you but you have to promise not to post it anywhere

↑ 4 ↓ Reply Share Report Save

Replayyy · 1 hour ago

Hey I don't know if you'll see this, but if you still have the link can I get it too? I won't post it. Thanks.

↑ 0 ↓ Reply Share Report Save

/u/LaceratedGrapes **here's the link you asked for**

[—] from LaceratedGrapes sent 3 mins ago

This is the entire last stream, so it's a big file. Here's the most relevant moments.

> 4:26:33 Just before
> 4:29:58 It happens
> 5:02:00 Possible witness
> 8:13:01 Body discovered

https://drive.google.com/drive/1-LlTywAruJXwH5xxzZ-rU8pqxzmdyGnDLj3

7://

She shouldn't watch it. No one should watch it. It shouldn't exist.

She's always avoided them before, those videos everyone knows are out there, floating in the void, traded around the most despicable nooks and chans. Executions. Skydiving accidents. Police bodycams.

Teresa doesn't want to watch this video. There's no doubt it will disturb and upset her. Just reading about Kyle's death was enough to do that.

Sometimes she thinks she is more porous than other people. Things that would bounce off a thicker skin go right through hers and lodge themselves deep inside her. She can't read the news with a detached interest. Can't become numb. She feels it all. Even as a kid, she'd cry herself to sleep over the suffering of some stranger she'd only heard about secondhand. It's not because she's a wonderful person or anything. It's almost rude, like she is stealing pain that doesn't belong to her. She'd stop if she could.

Becks was sensitive, too. She'd tear up when she saw a lost-cat poster. But somehow it didn't immobilize her, didn't blot out her joy. Becks didn't see the world as infinitely terrifying. She saw more good than bad. Teresa borrowed her optimism. She would bask in the reflected light of Becks's smile, like a pallid moon to her bright sun.

Teresa's hands are shaking before she even hits play.

Kyle's room is dark, his face lit only by computer screen glow. His camera is low quality, reducing his features to a ghoulish smear of pixels. He's playing a first-person shooter game that was popular a few years ago.

The file the stranger sent includes the whole stream start to finish— eight hours of video. Teresa skips ahead to the first time stamp provided in the message, labeled "Just before."

Lie25, aka Kyle, looks like so many other amateur streamers, his overlay an imitation of the more successful. He's got a subscription goal up in the corner, eight out of fifty subs achieved so far. On the right, the space he's designated for chat is empty. Just a gray box, the same shade as his shirt.

Teresa scrubs back to earlier in the stream, finds a stretch where the chat is active. One viewer says *hi* in chat, and Kyle carries on a short conversation, his part spoken aloud, theirs typed. Another viewer drops a link to their own channel, says *sub for sub*. Kyle had at least three viewers at one point, based on the chat log, though she can't see the actual numbers.

So much of finding an audience is luck—she knows that better than anyone—but she can't turn off the tiny, critical voice in the back of her mind. *He should get a better camera*, she thinks. *He should talk more*.

Then she remembers why she is watching this and feels guilty. None of that matters anymore, does it?

She drags herself back to the "Just before" time stamp. Kyle has gone almost entirely silent. Teresa's not familiar enough with this game to know if he's doing well or not. Someone tries to snipe him. He takes them out instead and mutters something under his breath, so faint that Teresa must pause, turn up the volume, play it back. She is rewarded for her trouble with "fucking bitch" so close to her ear it feels personal.

A few seconds later, Kyle dies in the game. He slams a hand on his desk. His keyboard jumps.

He gets up, opens the door to his room. The hallway is dark. He sort of melts into it, goes entirely out of view.

Shouldn't he at least say something? *Be right back?* Or put a video up on the screen to fill the dead space? It seems careless not to. Unless no one is watching anymore. Kyle would be able to see the viewer number.

He is gone for a minute and a half. Teresa times it, watching the runtime as the silence stretches on. There's a faint mechanical humming noise, probably his computer's fan whirring desperately to cool itself off. The room is too dark to make out much more than dim shapes in the background. Some large block that might be a dresser, with a jumble of smaller shapes atop it. Maybe action figures or those big-headed statues everyone likes. One looks like a trophy. Had Kyle run track? Played soccer? Shot targets? He was a real person once. A person with a whole life.

The sound of a door opening, closing.

Teresa turns to check her own door, just to be sure, but the sound was from the video. She turns back. Kyle reappears at the end of the hallway, a shadowy figure, moving forward. He's walking slowly. At the threshold of his room, he stumbles. Stands still for a moment, right in the doorway.

And then he falls.

She hears the *thump* of his body hitting the floor. He's almost out of frame, just a low shape at the bottom of the screen, a huddled darkness.

This has already happened. Months ago. There's nothing she can do. No way to change it. Teresa's pulse is racing nonetheless. She digs her nails into her palms. *Get up. Get back up.*

Becks? Get up.

She's reached the stranger's second time stamp—"It happens"— but she can't bring herself to skip ahead to the next one. She watches in real time. She feels unable to look away, her eyes glued to the shape on the floor. Is he still breathing? She can't tell.

Three long minutes pass. Teresa's not in her room, not in her body. She's just eyes, watching. She's in the computer, in the video.

Finally, the shape—Kyle—moves. And she's sorry she kept watching. It's not a good kind of movement. Jerky. Like he's being yanked around, pulled by unseen hands. Maybe he's having a seizure.

He's making a sound, too.

That's it. She can't take anymore. She pauses the video, minimizes the window.

She feels lightheaded when she stands, probably because she hasn't eaten yet today. She could open her door, get the bagel her father left outside. It would probably be slathered thick with cream cheese, the way she likes it.

She considers the mattress, which is leaning against the dresser, which is pushed in front of the door. Which is shut.

There's nothing out there, right? Just a hallway, just her house, just her parents and her brother. Rationally, she knows that she should remove all the stuff in front of the door. She should get the bagel. She should go down the hallway to the bathroom before she is forced to resort to using an empty water bottle.

She should go outside, even. At least to the backyard. The backyard is probably safe.

She knows all this.

But you can know something and not believe it.

After some rummaging, she finds a partially crushed granola bar under a pile of textbooks. There's one gulp of water left in the plastic bottle she keeps by her bed.

She returns to the computer, pulls up the clip of her own stream from the day before. She watches it through once. Hits replay. Watches it again, willing herself to notice something different this time, a giveaway, a tell, a logical explanation.

She watches it six times and doesn't find one.

So she opens the Kyle window again. Skips ahead a few minutes from where she left off. The body at the bottom of the frame is motionless again, the room silent. She skips ahead in five-minute increments until she hits the next time stamp the stranger gave her.

At first it seems like nothing has changed. She's so focused on the room, it takes her a moment to notice. Someone has spoken in chat. She'd assumed no one was watching this when it really happened. There'd been no reaction when Kyle fell, no acknowledgment that something was wrong.

There still isn't. The viewer is typing nonsense. A confusion of random letters.

The username is familiar, though.

It takes her another few moments to realize why.

 Replay is live now with 153 viewers
Category: Just Chatting
BRICK URGENT UPDATE

Replay looks rumpled, hair loose and lank. She keeps pushing a strand out of her eye. She is leaning toward the camera, talking fast.

The camera is shifted so that her bedroom door is no longer in frame. Now there is just the blank wall with taped-up flags.

> "Okay, look everyone, I'm streaming right now because I need your help. And because I need you all to believe me. I think Brick is in danger. Like really bad danger."

> ### Chat
>
> [0:55]—YOo
> [0:59]—u still haunted?

> "There's this guy, Lie25. This came up on my last stream, but I wasn't sure it was connected so I didn't really go into it."

> [1:07]—who?

> "His real name is Kyle. And he died. About six

months ago. I watched it. I watched him die."

[1:17]—what??

"Sorry, sorry, I'm telling this all wrong. He was streaming when he died. That's the point. He died onstream."

[1:21]—is this real?

She screenshares her browser, open to the news article about Kyle's death.

"Someone must have recorded it. Or maybe it's like how I have my account set to upload the VOD automatically as soon as I end stream. I don't know. It's been taken down now. If you go to his account, it's not there."

[1:59]—what does this have to do with Brick

"But someone saved it. I watched it."

[2:03]—show us!

"I wish I hadn't, but here's the thing—no, I'm not going to show you the video. Don't try to find it, okay? I think it was wrong to watch it. Like maybe it wasn't even safe. I don't know."

[2:14]—not fair

She darts a glance behind her as if she thinks there might be someone there.

"But okay, that's not . . . I just—"

[2:33]—I hope this stream gets weird

"Chat, this is serious. This guy, Kyle. He really died. This isn't a bit. I'm not faking any of this. I didn't fake my last stream."

[2:45]—lol yeah right

"As far as I can tell, there was only one person watching Kyle's stream when he died. I saw them talking in chat."

She switches from the article to a still of Brick's stream, the moment the donation showed on the screen:

Tjbnfskha donated $25: Open the door

[3:06]—open the door

"It was this guy. T-J-B-N-F-S-K-H-A. It was the same person. The same username."

[3:13]—ooh lore

"That's got to be more than a coincidence, doesn't it? Like, he was there when this guy dies and then he's there right before shit goes down with Brick. What are the chances of that?"

[3:17]—Brick's secret alt account?

She is talking very fast now. Speeding up by the sentence, really. She's not looking at the camera anymore. Her gaze flits around the room, settling now and then on the laptop just out of frame.

"Maybe he's some kind of digital hit man? Like he's figured out a fucked-up form of next-level swatting? Is that even possible?"

[3:21]—sounds like a conspiracy theory
[3:28]—you are off the deep end girl

The camera shakes a little. She's jiggling her leg, drumming her fingers on the top of the desk.

"No, no, you're right. That doesn't make sense.

And that's not even what I think is going on.
What I think is . . . well, what I think is that he's
not a *he*. I mean, maybe it's not a person at all."

[3:56]—wtf is she talkin about im lost
[4:01]—tell brick we said hi lol

"I don't know what it is, chat, I don't know. But
I think it killed Kyle. And I think it's trying to kill
Brick."

[4:06]—o_O

"If that's true, we've got to do something. We've
got to help him. We can't just sit back and watch.
Otherwise, if anything happens to him, it will be
our fault. If we just sit back and do nothing . . .
We have to prevent it. We have to stop it."

[4:14]—is she serious I can't tell
[4:15]—she is a good actor
[4:17]—Replay blink twice if you are
serious

She's breathing too fast. She stands up from the desk abruptly,
knocks over her own chair.

"I've sent him messages, but I don't think he

can access them right now."

[4:28]—proof they are working 2gether!

"You've seen him. He doesn't move. Like, I don't know if he's drugged or possessed or what."

[4:40]—brick is probably just high af
[4:45]—this is part of the ARG right?

She is pacing back and forth, going in and out of frame. She passes in front of the camera, going left. The view blurs as the camera tries to autofocus on the blank wall behind her. She passes by again, going the other way. But this time, after she sweeps out of frame, something has changed.

The wall behind her. It's not blank anymore.

Right in the center.

A door.

[4:51]—Holy shit
[4:56]—YES I knew it would get weird

She hasn't noticed anything yet. She's still talking and pacing.

[5:01]—Door!!
[5:03]—omg
[5:05]—open the door

"What we need is to find someone who knows him IRL and could go check on him. I've sent a bunch of messages, but I don't really know those people. And if they're not going to do it, we've got to do it ourselves. I found this."

[5:18]—Replay look behind you haha
[5:19]—open the doooorrrrr
[5:20]—open the door open the door

Replay returns to the desk. She leans over her laptop, clicks something. And then she sees what is behind her.

"Uh. Chat?"

She's gone stiff with fear, eyes wide. Her voice drops to a shaky whisper.

"Can you see that? Is that there? That shouldn't be there."

[5:54]—yes we can all see it

She turns her head slowly, reluctantly, to look behind her, at the place where there is clearly a door.

"It's not there. I swear, it's not. It's just on the screen."

[6:17]—FAKE
[6:20]—How is she doin it???
[6:20]—open the door!

Replay shakes her hands, violently as if they are wet, as if she is flinging water from them. She is breathing fast.

"No. No, this isn't happening. It's not there. I'm not opening it. I can't open it, chat, it's just a wall. There's no door."

The door looks real. It looks three dimensional. It has a brass knob, just like her other door. There is light coming through the gaps around the hinges.

[6:25]—Replay this is so cool
[6:26]—how did u come up with this?

"This isn't right. This isn't safe. I don't—"

She scrubs her face with her hands. Her chest is heaving. She squints at the feed, teeth clenched, glances at the wall, back to the feed. When she speaks it is between gasped breaths.

> "I'm not faking any of this. I'm not! I wish I was. And I don't think Brick is faking either. He's in danger, chat."

She pulls something new up on-screen. A Zillow listing for a house that is no longer for sale.

> [6:33]—don't show us houses we can't afford lol

> "I can't—"

Her voice hitches on a half sob. She shakes her head, clicks rapidly through several carefully staged photos, all the surfaces immaculate and shining. She stops on a bedroom.

> "I can't just leave him. Look. Look at this. Doesn't it look like the room Brick streams from?"

> [6:40]—Omg it does
> [6:42]—bruh is she doxxing rn?

She's made the feed from her own camera small again, moved it down to the corner. It's harder to see now, but the door is still there, still behind her.

You have to be looking very close to see this next part.

The doorknob is turning.

> "And see, this listing is in San Antonio. We know that's where Brick lives."

[6:46]—uh oh are there mods here?
[6:53]—yr gon get banned

It's turning very slowly, but there's no mistaking it.

[6:57]—replay watch out

> "I think this is his address. Someone needs to go there and—"

This channel is temporarily unavailable due to a violation of Community Guidelines or Terms of Service.

↑ **r/LivestreamFail** · Posted by user/moonpiepudding 30 mins ago

436

↓ **Streamer dies onstream??**

Brick copycat gets BANhammered midstream

https://clips.tv/:QuaintDeliciousBenchPotato-YR743UoH7XRVAjR

22 comments

mysonsaclown · 2 hours ago

Damn the mods worked fast on this one

↑ 987 ↓ Reply Share Report Save

> **Jaylinn_0** · 2 hours ago
>
> I bet this was planned
>
> ↑ 431 ↓ Reply Share Report Save

CatasterousNatterbox · 2 hours ago

Who TF is she?

↑ 608 ↓ Reply Share Report Save

> **TheCatNeverLeft** · 1 hour ago
>
> She used to do retro game playthroughs apparently. Never heard of her
>
> before this.
>
> ↑ 176 ↓ Reply Share Report Save

Latest Posts

Ash @Ashmunk23
I can't believe I even have to say this but doxxing people is NEVER okay

💬 0   🔁 2   ♥ 34

Isabel Christean (she/her) Reposted
Oranges R Evil @OrangesREvil
conclusive proof that the BrickARG and Replay streams are connected: a thread (1/9)

💬 9   🔁 12   ♥ 57

I Heart Brick @brickgirl1208
Remember everyone this is all FAKE. It is ACTING. Like I actually think it's kind of problematic for Brick and Replay not to make that clear to their viewers before someone takes things too far. Have we all just forgotten the made-of-cake murders?

💬 16   🔁 5   ♥ 421

Lyte-Vorb Hydration + Energy @lytevorb
Come thru for our Lemon Lime Electrolyte VR Experience!

💬 92   🔁 61   ♥ 605

What's happening

News · Trending
Flooding

#itstoolate
Trending with climate change

Noah Get the Boat

Gaming · Trending
KingCoal

Technology · Trending
AI Sues Creator

Who to follow

@briann832 . . . follows you

@Cronecat . . . follows you

@pogfrog . . . follows you

Sparklekitty
What the hell did you do
Please tell me you did not do what everyone is
saying
You are trending and not in a good way

there's something going on sparkle
i think Brick is in real danger
can you try to get in touch with Lil again?

Knock it off with that shit
Seriously, you sound unhinged
You need to make a statement
Take it all back
Try to do damage control

what, like an apology video?
everyone hates those

You are basically CANCELED

this is serious
i had to do something though
i couldn't just sit back and let it happen
he's in danger, I swear

The only danger to Brick right now is YOU
You doxxed him

That's never okay
I don't know if you're having some kind of
mental breakdown or what
But I can't let you drag other creators down
with you
your actions reflect on all of us
We can't tolerate toxic behavior in the group

are you kicking me out??
please dont sparkle
im just trying to do the right thing

Maybe you can join again when you get your
shit together

im sorry 😣

Ozma

shit
ozma i think i fucked up big-time

what? are you okay?
i'm getting off my shift in five

i got banned
violated TOS

oh dang

i really messed up

it's probably just a temporary ban, right?
remember brick got banned for like a week
last year

they should ban him again now
like for his own good
something really weird is going on
there was this other guy
and he died
and im scared
i think its all real
i think brick is in danger
he
i don't know
maybe I am too
i don't know
on my stream
there was this door
and there shouldn't be a door
there isn't a door
and just
i don't know what's happening

are you having a panic attack rn?

yes

8://

Ozma's voice is a tether. A bright thread Teresa can follow to escape the maze of her mind.

"Hey," says Ozma. "Just breathe in and out and, you know, all that basic-bitch healing-crystal shit. It's going to be okay, I promise."

Teresa can hear background noises. A crackle of wind. A car horn in the distance. "Are you outside?" she asks.

"Yeah, I literally called you the second I stepped out of work. I'm in the parking lot. What's going on?"

"I don't even know." Teresa is circling her room, phone clutched tight to her ear. She understands the ban. She crossed a line. What she doesn't understand is the door. How could it appear there on her wall, where no door should be? And why did it scare her so much?

Doors are good. They keep things in, keep things out. Keep your little brother from spying on you. Slow the progress of a house fire. People talk about opening doors to other worlds, to new possibilities, to the mind. Even the subconscious recognizes the significance of a door. You know that thing where you sometimes forget what you are looking for when you walk from room to room? Teresa read an article about it once. The brain stores a different set of memories and expectations for each room, and it recognizes a door as a threshold, a reflexive trigger to abandon whatever it was doing and prepare for something new.

"How did you get banned?" Ozma asks. "Nip slip?"

It's a joke but Teresa is too lightheaded to laugh. She feels herself peeling away from the moment, disassociating. She tries to stay grounded, focusing on her bare feet as they hit the floor, focusing on Ozma's voice. She loves the sound of Ozma's voice. It is lilting, musical.

"I-I figured out where Brick lives. I showed his house onstream."

"What?" Ozma sounds incredulous. "Why?"

Teresa hears the familiar clanks and rustles of Ozma getting into the car. Teresa has never seen it, but she can picture it. A beat-up little gray sedan, paint peeling. Ozma is eighteen—only a year older than Teresa—but her life is wildly different. She goes outside. She drives. She has her own place.

Well, kind of her own place. Really, it's her cousin's house and her cousin's car that he lets her use when he's out of town. He's a long-haul trucker, so he's gone most of the time.

"I felt like I had to do something," says Teresa. "He's in danger. Everyone thinks I'm making things up or just trying to get attention or . . ."

She was going to say they think she's crazy, but that's the thing, isn't it? She *is* crazy, technically speaking. Certified mentally ill.

That doesn't mean she isn't right.

"I'm sorry," she says instead. She takes a deep breath. "I need to slow down. How are you? How was work?"

"Work was a French vanilla hellscape like always. This one lady made a point of calling me *young man* for no reason."

"Ugh. That's bullshit."

"It is, but whatever. She was, like, super old."

Ozma only recently came out at work. She's not out yet to her family. Online is the only place, she's told Teresa, where she feels like people truly see her the way she is.

A few weeks ago, she and Teresa watched *Return to Oz* together, playing it at the same time while on a call together. In the film, Princess Ozma rescues Dorothy from an asylum, and then later Dorothy frees Ozma from the mirror where she's been imprisoned. The villains are super campy. The bearded Nome King steals and wears the ruby slippers. The witch Mombi steals the heads of pretty girls to keep in glass cabinets, so she can wear them when she wants. According to Ozma, in the original book, Mombi curses the character of Princess Ozma, transforming her for years into the shape of a boy. That's where Ozma got her username, which she eventually decided to take as her real name too.

"If I was there," says Teresa, "I would have punched that lady, no matter how old and crusty she was."

Ozma laughs. "You'd get me fired."

"Well, I got myself banned, so maybe that's just my thing now."

"Okay, seriously though, are you okay?"

Teresa hears the rumble of the car starting. This always makes her tense. She's worried that she'll distract Ozma from the road, but Ozma promises that she keeps her phone in the holder and never touches it or looks at it while driving. Teresa has told Ozma about the accident. She's the only one of her online friends who knows.

Teresa takes a deep breath.

"I just wish I could be calm," she says, trying hard to keep a hitch out of her voice, "even for a moment."

"Yeah," says Ozma. "You deserve that."

That hits Teresa hard somehow. Not because she thinks Ozma is right.

Because she thinks she's wrong.

How can Teresa deserve to relax, how can she deserve anything, when she doesn't even deserve to be alive? It should have been her who died that night. Becks should still be here.

Teresa had told Becks once that she didn't always feel like a girl. It was on one of their drives. Not that final one. This time it was still light out. They'd parked at a trailhead and walked into the forest. Away from everything but the silent trees, it felt like conventional rules of the world no longer applied.

Teresa has since told Ozma. And Jolley. But Becks was the first. After Teresa told her, she'd smiled and said *cool* and *that makes sense* and *you're like a secret agent but for gender roles*. She was so good. So full of life and kindness. If Teresa could trade her own life for Becks's, she would do it in an instant.

Someone pounds on the door. So loud and sudden that Teresa drops the phone. It hits the floor and skitters away like an enormous black insect.

"Teresa?" Her mother's voice, muffled through the door and the dresser and mattress.

Teresa is down on her knees, scrabbling to retrieve her phone. She checks the time. Her mom is home from work early. Is something wrong?

"I'm so, so sorry," she says into the phone, breathless. "My mom is here, can I call you later?"

"Yeah, no problem," says Ozma. "I have a lot of questions, but for what it's worth, I don't think you're making it all up."

"Thanks," Teresa says, and feels a warm glow at Ozma's words. A brief flame of comfort, snuffed out at once by a new round of door hammering.

She hangs up and goes to the door.

"What?" she shouts.

"Can you open the door, honey?"

Teresa is pretty sure she is never going to open another door again in her life. Her phone is still in her hands, so she calls her mother's cell. She hears it ring out in the hallway.

"This is ridiculous," her mom says when she finally answers the phone. "I'm right here, just open the door and talk to me."

"It's easier this way," Teresa says. "We don't have to shout."

"I can't just let you do this," her mom says.

How are you going to stop me? Teresa thinks, but she says nothing.

"Dr. Kole has agreed to an emergency session. He's going to call in ten."

"I don't need—"

"If you don't at least do this, Teresa, I'll have to get your father to take the door off the hinges."

So Teresa agrees.

She huddles in the farthest corner from the door, safe in a temporary fort formed from a sheet draped over her head. As a kid she'd burrow under her blankets and pretend they were arctic caves. Maybe she's too old for that now, but she doesn't care. The sheets tint all the light filtering into her cave an aqueous blue. She is safe. No one can reach her here.

Well, except her therapist. His face peers out from the glowing rectangle of her phone.

Teresa is trying to explain to him why she can't open her bedroom door. There's no way around it. She has to tell him the whole story— Brick, the shadowy figure, the door that appeared from nowhere.

She can see it in his eyes, what he thinks of all this. She knows what to expect even before he says it, in a gentle, cautious tone, as though she is a wounded animal he is trying not to frighten.

Delusions, he says.

Paranoia, he says.

She tries to insist, offers to send him the videos as proof, but he isn't interested in that. He doesn't really understand streaming. He thinks it is another unhealthy coping mechanism.

Teresa likes her therapist. She is thankful for him. Some of the things he said, in the early days after the accident, managed to permeate the thick cocoon of her pain. He spoke to her about respecting the process of grief, about letting yourself feel it, *welcome* it, even. He told her that the goal is not to "get over it." The pain will never truly be gone, but the shape of it will change with time. You will learn to live alongside it.

But these days she feels like his counsel too often boils down to "go touch grass," and honestly her parents could save a ton of money by just hiring any random internet commenter instead.

He is asking her a series of insistent questions, now.

Does she feel unsafe? Well, yes.

Is she going to hurt herself? No.

Is she going to hurt someone else? No.

But she's worried someone will die.

"If something happened to this guy, it wouldn't be your fault," her therapist says. "Remember, you don't actually know him."

Which is true. She's never spoken to Brick. He has no idea she exists.

But in another sense, she *does* know him, with a degree of intimacy usually reserved for close family or friends. She knows his favorite food, his most vivid childhood memories, his greatest fears. She knows the sound of his laugh, how his eyes crinkle at the corners when he smiles, the way he chews on the lower-left corner of his lip when he is concentrating.

"Anyway," her therapist goes on, leaning forward into his camera, "even if you did know him, it wouldn't be your fault."

"Yeah, but I can't just stand by and—"

"Rebecca's death was not your fault," he says, cutting her off.

"I know."

"I want to hear you say it."

Teresa sighs. "It wasn't my fault."

She knows that, but she doesn't for a second *believe* it.

 Brick is live now with 9K viewers
Category: Just Chatting
OPEN THE DOOR

Brick is sitting at his desk. The same place he's been sitting the last day and a half.

His skin has taken on a sallow complexion. Sweat is beading along his hairline. His eyes are bloodshot, ringed in faint purple.

He looks ill. He looks like a man who has not slept in at least twenty-four hours, which he demonstrably hasn't. He's been live for the last twenty-eight hours. Awake, staring.

> ### Chat
> [28:45:01]—has anyone else been here the whole stream?
> [28:45:18]—I have
> [28:45:23]—yeah right

The sound of muffled knocking starts up in the background. Far-off. Maybe the front door.

Brick doesn't react.

> [28:45:52]—does everyone hear that?

[28:46:04]—finally something happening!

The knocking continues for some time, then gives way to a rasping sound, like a key in a lock.

Footsteps. Coming closer.

A voice, faint, calls out from the distance. "Hello?"

[28:46:19]—who is that?
[28:46:32]—maybe his mommy comin to check on him
[28:46:39]—MOM REVEAL

The sound of a door opening and shutting.

And then a louder knock. This one seemingly on the bedroom door.

The voice comes again.

"Hello? Brick?"

It is a female voice. A voice familiar to some.

[28:46:57]—no wait, listen
[28:47:00]—is that her?

[28:47:16]—omg no way

"I'm coming in."

The door opens.

Framed in the doorway, a figure, but not made of shadow. A girl, very pretty, her black hair tied back in a ponytail. She's got less makeup on than usual, no bright wig, but her face is still instantly recognizable.

[28:47:28]—WhomegaLil!!!
[28:47:37]—hi Lil!
[28:47:38]—they are so totally dating

She steps hesitantly into the room, her eyes fixed on the figure in the computer chair.

The door is open behind her, but the hallway light is on. No room for shadows.

"Brick? Can you hear me?"

Brick doesn't move, doesn't react.

[28:47:55]—dude she had a key to his place
[28:48:00]—sus as hell

Lil approaches him. She places a hand on his shoulder, shakes him gently, crouches down to look into his eyes. She glances at the camera once, then back at Brick. She whispers, almost inaudibly.

"Nick? Are you okay?"

Brick doesn't respond.

[28:48:06]—she used his real name!
[28:48:07]—W rizz
[28:48:08]—such a cute couple <3

Lil turns to the camera again.

"Chat. I'm not sure what's going on, exactly, but I'm going to end stream now and get him some help."

[28:48:12]—don't end!!!

She reaches forward, over Brick, for the mouse.

Brick moves.

It is sudden and violent. He jerks in his chair. His arm shoots out, knocking the keyboard aside and grabbing her wrist.

[28:48:24]—whoa

[28:48:31]—holy shit
[28:48:39]—clip this clip this!!

Lil stumbles back.

"What are you doing? Nick?"

The screen goes black.

[28:48:45]—wait is the stream over?
[28:48:53]—what just happened
[28:48:53]—O-O

We can still hear noises.

A clatter. Things falling off the desk, maybe.

[28:49:04]—im so confused
[28:49:18]—is it over?

Lil shouts, but the sound is muffled, cut short.

[28:49:32]—whats happenin
[28:49:35]—they are prob making out

A loud *slam*.

Another *slam*.

[28:49:49]—did I miss something?
[28:49:52]—What's going on

A heavy *thump*.

[28:49:55]—well this is awkward
[28:49:49]—is the stream broken?

Silence.

[28:50:11]—ResidentSleeper
[28:50:34]—F?

Silence.

[28:50:47]—naptime
[28:51:01]—Lil n Brick just wanted
some privacy lolol
[28:51:10]—zZZzZ

And then the picture returns suddenly, popping back into vivid life
with no transition.

[28:51:40]—yay!
[28:51:42]—pogchamp

Brick sits in his computer chair just as before, facing forward, staring into the camera.

> [28:51:49]—he back
> [28:52:01]—normality has returned

Behind him, the door is still open, the hallway light is off, the doorframe filled again with a hazy darkness.

> [28:52:03]—uh oh hallway
> [28:52:15]—ghost time?
> [28:52:30]—where is Lil
> [28:52:33]—lil?

He is alone.

> [28:52:42]—F

r/BrickARG · Posted by user/Ghan42 10 minutes ago

↑

56 **Look at this screenshot I am seriously freaked out**

↓

https://imgr.com/a/LEt%xJ5cXW

12 comments

ConfusedMedKid · 10 minutes ago

what am I supposed to be looking at? It's just brick.

↑ **47** ↓ Reply Share Report Save

Ghan42 · 9 minutes ago

In the lower left corner

↑ **11** ↓ Reply Share Report Save

ConfusedMedKid · 9 minutes ago

What I still don't see it

↑ **2** ↓ Reply Share Report Save

Ghan42 · 7 minutes ago

Here I've circled it for you

https://imgr.com/Qgvsx?YOu90

↑ **22** ↓ Reply Share Report Save

ConfusedMedKid · 6 minutes ago

. . . oh shit

↑ **4** ↓ Reply Share Report Save

stranglingfruit · 4 minutes ago

Wtf is that a shoe?

↑ 8 ↓ Reply Share Report Save

> **BrianJRocks** · 3 minutes ago
>
> I think it might be, like just the edge of it, poking in from out of frame
>
> ↑ 4 ↓ Reply Share Report Save

> > **stranglingfruit** · 2 minutes ago
> >
> > the angle is weird
> >
> > ↑ 1 ↓ Reply Share Report Save

brickpoggers · 4 minutes ago

That definitely wasn't there before

↑ 6 ↓ Reply Share Report Save

> **Ghan42** · 3 minutes ago
>
> You're right, here's from fifteen minutes earlier
>
> https://imgr.com/%D0wn63QXI2
>
> ↑ 14 ↓ Reply Share Report Save

> > **BrianJRocks** · 2 minutes ago
> >
> > It shows up right after the black screen at 28:48:50
> >
> > ↑ 12 ↓ Reply Share Report Save

loverofwriting123 · 2 minutes ago

Do you think that's Lil?????

↑ -2 ↓ Reply Share Report Save

KingCoal is live now with 6.7K viewers
Category: Block Game
XSMP—CHILL BASE BUILDING STREAM

KingCoal, a young man in a striped sweater, is building the roof of an enormous cathedral-like structure out of digital blocks. He is British Indian, with dark curly hair and sharp cheekbones. He sits in front of a green screen, so that his head and shoulders appear to float in the bottom-left corner, superimposed above the gameplay.

> "Thanks for the five gifted, FloridaFlamingoGirl. You're a rockstar!"

Chat

[13:33]—hi hi hi
[13:34]—im getting too many ads

He places a block, breaks a block.

> "I'm not sure about this roof color. Maybe we want to try some acacia as an accent?"

[13:48]—I wish I could build this good
[13:50]—my stuff looks like trash

He jumps to the ground, catching himself at the last moment with a water bucket. He walks through an archway lit by torches and into the grand entrance hall of the building.

Lanterns hang from the ceiling on long chains. The windows are stained glass. The walls are decorated with a repeating gradient pattern of gray and white blocks.

He clicks open a small wooden door on the left and steps into a smaller room. The walls here are lined with wooden chests. He opens one, selects some blocks from inside.

The screen goes dark, then flashes back, then goes dark again.

[14:03]—open the door

KingCoal grumbles.

"Server is acting up."

He opens a chat window in the game. Types. We can see the earlier messages in the chat.

```
<LifeWithWaffles> hit the ground too hard
<LifeWithWaffles> lol whoops
<King_Coal> joined the game
<LifeWithWaffles> Hey hey:)
<King_Coal> im live
```

```
<Tjbnfskha> joined the game
<LifeWithWaffles> who is that?
<Tjbnfskha> left the game
<King_Coal> Anybody else's game
glitching out?
```

[14:56]—wats goin on
[14:58]—this stream is so scuffed

In the game, KingCoal selects more blocks from a chest, then turns and opens the little wooden door. But it no longer leads to the grand entrance hall.

"What?"

Beyond the door is a narrow hallway made of gray stone. The light from the storage room only reaches about ten blocks in or so. Beyond that it is dark.

KingCoal does a double take in the game, his view whipping back and forth.

"This is so weird. Was this Waffles? I mean, it must be. She's the only one on the server right now. How did she build this so fast without me noticing?"

[15:06]—creepy

[15:08]—lol pranked

"I don't even understand how this is here." He tries breaking the blocks just beside the door, but beyond them is more gray stone. "I mean, I guess I've got to at least check it out, don't I?"

[15:11]—nope nope nope
[15:12]—omg don't go in there

KingCoal laughs. It's only a game, after all.

He steps in.

Horsegirl4 is live now with 4.8K viewers
Category: Survival Game
NEW MAPS LET'S SEE HOW LONG WE CAN HOLD OUT

A person in a full-face rubber horse mask and a black sweatshirt sits in front of a wall checkerboarded with foam sound-dampener panels. To their right is a large potted monstera plant, clearly fake. To their left, a golden horse statue.

In the game they are running through a field of dead grass toward a house that looks abandoned.

> **Chat**
>
> [17:55]—Runnnnnn

A shot rings out.

"Ha! You missed."

> [17:58]—LUL
> [18:02]—they shoot worse than I do

They reach the house, click through the front door, dart inside.

"My house now. Anyone in here better clear out quick."

They speak in a slight Scandinavian accent. Their voice is artificially deep, clearly modulated through a voice changer.

We can't see their expression through the mask. No one online, in fact, has ever seen their real face.

[18:17]—horse house
[18:20]—yeye

They race through the house, dipping in and out of empty rooms. In the kitchen, they click open weathered cabinets. In the bathroom, they check the grimy tub.

"Give me something. Anything. Shotgun would be great."

Out in the hallway again. Another figure passes by the doorway at the end of the hall.

Horsegirl darts back into the bathroom and shuts the door.

"Was that a player? It was too dark to tell."

[19:11]—hide in the bathtub lol
[19:13]—Open the door

A shot rings out but it is far in the distance, somewhere outside the house.

"I don't think they saw me. Let's run."

They click back through the bathroom door and dart down the hallway.

> [19:34]—r u even a girl irl?
> [19:36]—I bet not

They turn a corner, but then abruptly stop short. Their view in the game is pointed down at the intersection of a grainy brown floor and a pixelated white wall.

Something moves in the corner of the screen. A shadow.

> [19:40]—watch out!!

It is perfectly silent. No gunshots. No clack of keyboard. Horsegirl is not moving, either in real life or the game. It seems to be getting darker. In real life and in the game.

> [19:41]—wtf run
> [19:41]—everyone knows horsegirl is secretly ur mom

The flat black eyes of the horse mask betray no emotion.

9://

Teresa's mind is spiderwebbed out, spinning new threads every minute. She dips in and out of an article about hauntings. Another article on cybersecurity. A Google alert pings continually for new posts about Brick. Little rectangles, crowding every corner of her screen. Little windows.

She's monitoring four livestreams, clicking quick between them. Brick, KingCoal, Horsegirl, and Hedgelord. The latter three are all acting like Brick did in the beginning. Motionless, staring at the camera.

Or probably staring at the camera, in the case of Horsegirl. There's no way to tell with the mask, but they certainly aren't moving.

Teresa desperately wants to go live. She wants to be Replay instead of Teresa. She needs the energy of her viewers, needs the high. She can almost feel them, like a phantom limb. Phantom eyes.

But she's banned. Cut off from that lifeline. Cut off from the Rainbros chat, too. She's getting smeared on social media for doxxing Brick. The angry messages and mentions have become a raging flood.

The one bright spot is her clip channel. Her subscriber and viewer counts have both absolutely skyrocketed in the last few hours.

She was the first to post a clip of the moment KingCoal stopped speaking. Same with Horsegirl. She didn't get one of the moment Hedgelord stopped talking, but only because he started his stream already silent and staring. That's how Brick did it too, of course. Does that mean something? Teresa isn't sure.

She's kept up with posting Brick clips. Compilations and high-lights of the odd things he's been saying. She feels a little conflicted each time she hits the post button. Is it exploitative to share these clips? To gain subscribers from them?

But she's not doing it just for the numbers. It's part of solving the mystery. That's how she can justify it to herself. She can't figure everything out on her own. She doesn't know how to save Brick or the others. She needs help from viewers. She needs more people to watch, to see what she's seeing. She needs more eyes on the problem.

She checks in with the official fan server to see what people are saying there.

Brick House
Public
#copycats

magenta5
i think this supports the idea that its fake.
they are all friends

banana-n-oatmeal
hedgelord and brick aren't friends, are they?

magenta5
they definitely used to be

Replay
brick distanced himself publicly after
hedge's big takequake in the fall
but he never actually condemned hedge
or anything

magenta5
im still disappointed in that honestly

Replay
me too
anyway to me it doesn't make it seem
like faking
it makes it seem like contagion

magenta5
none of them even live in the same state,
do they?

eclipsedmoon
king and brick were both at BitChick's party
last month i saw the snaps

Replay
maybe its not a physical thing
the brick thing started after a dono too
"open the door" right

eclipsedmoon
right

Replay
well in king and horse's streams there was no
dono
but someone in chat says it
"open the door"
for king it was 1 minute 5 seconds before he
freezes
for horse, 45 seconds

magenta5
damn
you are thorough

banana-n-oatmeal
so what, that's like a code?
like something they all agreed on ahead of
time?

Replay
maybe
the one thing is that hedge doesn't fit the
pattern
did anyone watch his last stream before this
current one?

magenta5

not me

Replay

i can't find a vod

catandwrite

I saw part of it

Replay

did he open a door?

catandwrite

no he was just sitting at his desk

Replay

any door?

a door in a game?

catandwrite

I don't think so

he was mostly doing reacts

Replay

hmm okay thanks

eclipsedmoon

hey wait are you the same replay who tried to

> dox brick???
> that was really messed up
> you shouldn't even be here

Teresa sits back and rubs her eyes. Sometimes when she's on the computer she forgets she has a body. It's a rude shock when she is forced to remember.

She checks her phone. There's a new text from Ozma. Teresa's afraid to read it. Ozma will be home by now. She'll have had time to see the online backlash, time to talk to Sparkle. What if she's angry, too? What if she hates Teresa now? Teresa doesn't like feeling hated by strangers, but she'd take a million furious commenters wielding pitchforks over the thought of alienating Ozma any day.

It's strange, to think they've known each other for less than a year. It feels like longer. Her friendship with Ozma is different from the one she had with Becks, of course. There can never be a replacement. She worries sometimes that thinking of Ozma as her best friend would be a betrayal. She's afraid, also, of getting too close, of caring too much. It's probably too late for that. She cares about Ozma a lot. She thinks about her all the time. After they watched *Return to Oz*, Teresa kept imagining the two of them as the main characters. She the plain, brown-haired farm girl and Ozma the resplendent blond princess bringing magic back into her life.

She wishes she could introduce Ozma to Becks someday. Wishes they could all hang out together.

But wishing only makes it worse. She reads the text.

Ozma
everything okay there?

any more shadowy figures?

not yet

If only she could see Ozma's face. Hear her voice. Is she teasing? Is she worried? Is she annoyed?

ozma do you believe me?

do you believe it was real

Um

Teresa's stomach drops.

i wasn't faking it

i really wasn't

you swear you weren't?

i swear

then I believe you

getting some dinner and then I was going to stream but I'll call you again afterward, yeah?

we can talk it all through

Teresa spends a long moment reading and rereading those last few messages, trying to feel reassured. A few weeks ago, she and Ozma had kept talking so late they both fell asleep while still on the call. Lying in bed with her phone resting on her ear, Teresa could almost imagine that Ozma was there in the room with her. Almost imagine she was lying beside her. In that moment, she'd felt safe.

She does not feel safe now.

She's got to figure out what is happening to Brick before it spreads any further, before it gets any worse. The user who donated to Brick, Tjbnfskha, seems to be a connecting factor. That account follows all the streamers who've been affected so far.

Well, except for her. Teresa still doesn't understand what kept her from going catatonic after she saw the shadowy figure. Was it a fluke? Or just a delayed reaction? Will it catch up to her eventually?

She's got far more questions than answers. Who is Tjbnfskha? Why did they ask Brick to open the door? Why did they watch Kyle die and do nothing?

Did they do nothing? Or was Kyle their first victim?

Teresa can't find anything, any other traces of Tjbnfskha online, but Kyle—just like Becks—left evidence of himself behind online after he died. He used the same Lie25 username on multiple platforms, so Teresa has been tracking down all his old posts and comments, looking for clues.

Ding. Teresa switches tabs. Another article about Brick on a gaming news website.

Ding. A new private message. Another death threat from an angry Brick fan.

Thud. A sound from the real world this time, not her computer.

Teresa spins around. It's her door again.

Thud.

The whole blockade in front of the door shakes. The mattress shifts, starts to slide down.

Teresa jumps up from her desk and rushes over to catch the mattress. She pushes it back, trying to reinforce her defenses. Her heart is racing, but then again, it hasn't really slowed down in hours, so that's hardly a change. Everything is dangerous all the time. It never stops and it never gets better.

Thud.

↑
16
↓

r/streamersanonymous · Posted by user/Lie25 1 year ago

double standard??!

It's getting ridiculous. I can't get any views while working my ass off, streaming

for hours, playing my heart out, and then all these female streamers have to do is

wear a string bikini next to like a tiny cup of water and the mods let it fly as a hot

tub stream. It's such bullshit. Guess I'll just lay down and rot.

9 comments

Yerarockstarharry · 1 year ago

talent is rare but tits are common

↑ 20 ↓ Reply Share Report Save

CatasterousNatterbox · 1 year ago

I bet you're subbed to all of them

↑ 18 ↓ Reply Share Report Save

> **Lie25** · 1 year ago
>
> hell no thos btches aren't getting a dime
>
> ↑ -5 ↓ Reply Share Report Save

> > **Kurokubu** · 1 year ago
> >
> > he watches for free then
> >
> > ↑ 10 ↓ Reply Share Report Save

grumpmump · 1 year ago

beat em at their own game do your next stream in nothing but your natural

neckbeard and a bikini

↑ 14 ↓ Reply Share Report Save

glasshalfbanana · 1 year ago

Id fap to it

↑ **-3** ↓ Reply Share Report Save

> **Anhedoniana** · 1 year ago
>
> yes officer this comment right here
>
> ↑ **6** ↓ Reply Share Report Save

little_gnora · 1 year ago

the loopholes are admittedly getting way out of hand

↑ **6** ↓ Reply Share Report Save

> **Lie25** · 1 year ago
>
> THANK YOU this fucking site is full of simps
>
> ↑ **-7** ↓ Reply Share Report Save

↑
5
↓

Brick really let me down

Fuck him, man. I used to be a big fan. Like I was there from the start, back when he had way less viewers than he has these days. I've been subbed from day one basically. I have given him so much money over the years. I did it because I was a fan, but then I give him a donation with just a tiny plug for my stream ONE TIME and he doesn't read it. Just skips right over it. Like what the fuck. Aren't bigger streamers supposed to support the littler guys???? What about that stream where he would go to a streamer with zero views and donate 500 dollars? You know I am a loyal fan. When I think of how much I've given him over the years, when I've had a little extra here or there, it has been much more than five hundred dollars. I used to think he cared about his community but now I think he is just feeding off us. I'm so disappointed.

4 comments

comicsansserif320 · 1 year ago

I get you, at least partway. It does sometimes seem like when streamers blow up they forget about the fans who were with them from the start.

↑ 9 ↓ Reply Share Report Save

Diamond12Special · 1 year ago

He gets so many donations he can't read them all man

↑ 7 ↓ Reply Share Report Save

> **Lie25** · 1 year ago
>
> it really seemed like he skipped this one on purpose and like it would

be so easy for him to just read this one little thing and it could open the door to real growth for me

↑ -6 ↓ Reply Share Report Save

AllTheThingsSheSays · 1 year ago

That's just how streaming works. It's parasites all the way down.

↑ 5 ↓ Reply Share Report Save

← **Message requests** • • •

Kayleigh @kle674gurl   1m
Fuck you replay

Matt Is Working @Mp3p0-op   1m
I am going to track you down and . . .

Frogger @fr0ggeere_2   2m
Sent you a photo

Paul Cook @paulsezthings   2m
Hope someone doxxes you too

Mai Gardener @Mai_Gardener   2m
If anything happens to brick it is . . .

Brick is best @brick84_738   3m
JFC YOU SHOULD BE ASHAMED . . .

May XX @may_XxXxXx   4m
you deserve to die

Kayleigh @kle674gurl   4m
reply to me you coward

Terra Mistake @gmeee   4m
Sent you a photo

Matt Is Working @Mp3p0-op   5m
Your address isn't that hard to . . .

Tjbnfskha @Tjbnfskha   5m
hello

10://

Thud.

"Get the hell out here!"

It's her brother, shouting from the hallway. Teresa didn't expect that. Her mother again, yes. A shadow demon, maybe. But Jason?

Another *thud*. He is kicking the door. Hard. She can feel the jolt through the mattress.

"I thought you didn't have a sister!" she shouts back.

"Just come out here!" He sounds mad.

"I can't!" she shouts.

"You can. You just don't want to."

It's not true. She knows it's not true, but it still hurts to hear him say it. She'd love to be able to open the door without fear, to go downstairs, go outside. "Jason, I'm sorry. I really can't."

He kicks the door one more time. Then silence. Teresa presses her ear to the mattress. Has he left?

When he speaks again, it is in a quiet voice. "Fine," he says, "then let me in." He sounds much younger than fifteen for a moment, like the Jason she used to know, the little brother who would follow her around everywhere, begging to be included in whatever she was doing.

"Okay," she says. "Okay. Just stop kicking my door." She pulls the mattress down and pushes the dresser aside.

Jason bursts into the room before Teresa is out of the way. The door clips her shoulder and nearly knocks her over.

Jason doesn't seem to notice. He's planted himself in the center of the room and he's staring at the wall. The one behind her desk.

Teresa makes herself glance out of the open bedroom door. She sees nothing but the hallway, the familiar shapes and shadows. The open mouth of the stairs, the white banisters like rows of teeth.

The bagel her father brought earlier is still sitting on a plate on the floor. Teresa grabs it and then closes the door, hands shaking. Her shoulder throbs where it hit her.

"Jason?" she asks.

He turns. "Some kid from my class sent me a link," he says. "There's a fucking *news* article about you!"

"Jason! Language." She cringes as soon as the words leave her mouth. She sounds like their mother. Jason doesn't usually talk like that, though. He's always been a Goody Two-shoes. The well-behaved one. The normal one.

"Everyone at school was talking about it," he says. He is angry, glowering. He's taller than her. Has he grown since last time she saw him? Is that even possible? Maybe. He hit his growth spurt earlier this year, went from little boy to a gangly teen in the blink of an eye.

"Sorry," she says. What else can she say?

"How did you do it? Make the door show up?" He gestures at the wall behind the desk. "Was it prerecorded?"

"I didn't do anything."

"Liar."

"I swear I didn't. It just showed up. I'm not sure how. I think . . ."

She trails off. Should she tell him about Kyle, about what she thinks might be happening, though she has a hard time believing it herself? Would he believe her?

"You're saying it was real?" His tone is mocking. "A fake door just appeared on your wall? Is it still there? Is it invisible?"

He moves over to the wall as he talks, mimes feeling for a door. Pretends to find it, pretends to pull it—

"Don't!" She feels so silly, but she can't help herself.

The door isn't there. The door isn't real.

Jason rolls his eyes. "You've got to be so over the top about everything, don't you?"

"Sorry," she says again. She doesn't know how to talk to Jason anymore. It used to be easy. Even their fights were familiar when they were younger. Their roles were clear. She was the wise old leader, lording her lofty two-year advantage over him, and he was the often-annoying follower. But it's gotten all mixed up. He doesn't look up to her anymore, in either sense of the word.

She knows that began even before the accident, but it's gotten worse lately. She remembers one evening, a few weeks ago. She was still going downstairs at that point, though usually just long enough to grab some food. This evening her mother had insisted they all have dinner as a family, so she stayed longer and sat at the dining room table.

She had just speared a limp green bean with her fork when a car backfired outside. She was out of her seat in an instant, nerves jangling, every alarm in her mind and her body screaming *Danger*. She knocked over a water glass in her haste. Her mother jumped up and ran to comfort her. Her father stood, too, tried to soak up the spilled water with a napkin.

Jason alone stayed in his seat. He stared across the table at Teresa, face twisted in disgust. She felt certain, in that moment, that he hated her.

"Are you going to kill yourself?" Jason asks, now.

"What?" It's such an unexpected question that it startles her out of her spiral. "No."

An expression flits briefly across his face. Worry? Maybe it's still just anger. She can't tell.

"Mom and Dad think you're going to hurt yourself or something," he says, kicking at her fallen mattress. "I'm supposed to keep an eye on you because they've got some stupid theater thing they don't want to miss tonight, but you're too crazy to be left alone. So I guess I'm your fucking babysitter now."

"You don't have to . . ." Teresa feels a flood of shame. She used to look out for *him*. *She* was the protector. She can't protect anything now. "I won't hurt myself. I promise."

"You've got to leave your door open," says Jason.

Teresa squeezes her eyes shut. She hates that her little brother is in this position, hates that her parents asked him to do it. It's not fair. She knows that. She should try to make this easier on him.

And yet.

Brick saw the shadowy figure and then he went catatonic. She saw the shadowy figure, too, but she's not catatonic. Not yet, anyway. Why not? What did they do differently?

She didn't open the door.

"I can't," she says.

"Bullshit," he spits out.

Maybe she's wrong. Maybe it's nothing to do with doors. Maybe she simply turned off her laptop fast enough. Maybe this is another compulsion, another irrational fear.

But she can't make herself do it. She is trying, she is imagining it. Open the door. Open the door. Could she do it? Such a simple thing, right? But just the thought fills her with dread. Her hands are shaking again.

"For fuck's sake," says Jason, noticing her hands. "You've just been getting worse and worse. I don't think you're even trying to get better."

"I'm trying!"

"Then leave your room. Come downstairs. Be a normal fucking person."

She looks at him. What can she possibly say? She'd give him a window into her brain if she could, let him see how hard she is trying every minute of every day. Trying to exist, trying not to fall apart. Trying not to hurt anyone more than she already has.

They stare each other down. She feels tears threatening. Jason gives in first, turning away with a sound of disgust.

"Whatever," he says, "just don't block it then."

"Okay."

"If you kill yourself, I'll never forgive you." He leaves as abruptly as he entered, pushing Teresa aside and wrenching the bedroom door back open. He stomps away down the staircase.

Teresa hesitates.

She should do what her therapist says. Focus on what's here, on what's real. Focus on Jason instead of Brick. She should run down the stairs. Hug her little brother. Or maybe punch him in the arm for being so rude.

Instead, she closes the door.

Not all the way. She stops with just a sliver of space between door and frame. It's a compromise. A loophole. If it isn't closed, then she can't possibly open it, right?

Her phone dings. A notification. Ozma has gone live. She pulls up the stream while she eats her slightly stale bagel. Just the sight of Ozma's face is enough to make her feel a little less alone. Normally she might hop on a call, chat with Ozma onstream, but now that would violate the ban.

She almost wishes her brother would come back, even just to yell at her more. She misses him, misses spending time with him.

When she and Jason were younger, their parents had been super strict about screen time. Nothing digital past seven p.m. on a school night. So they'd had to get creative. There's a window in the attic that faces the same direction as the one in Teresa's bedroom, though the view is even better up there, unrestricted by powerlines. You could see basically every house on the street, even see right into the windows of some of them, catching glimpses of living rooms and kitchens and bedrooms.

"Let's see what's on channel one," Teresa would say. Every house was a different channel. Most of the time nothing was happening, but that just made the tiniest hint of movement or activity thrilling.

Teresa would narrate the shows for Jason.

"Here we see neighbor #3 emerging from their house," she'd say, putting on a nature-documentary British accent. "They stoop to tie their shoes. Peculiar behavior. Who leaves the house without tying their shoes first? Clearly what we have here is an alien in disguise."

Jason loved it. He'd fall over giggling, beg her to do more.

Teresa glances out her bedroom window, now. Channels one and two are both still and silent, the windows dark. On channel three, there's a lighted window.

Movement catches her eye down in the alleyway.

There's a person there, right across from her window. Not walking a dog. Not walking at all. They are standing in shadow, so she can't make out the details of their face, but she can tell they are facing this way. Staring up at her house.

Staring right at her.

 Ozma is live now with 135 viewers
Category: Life Game
COZY COTTAGECORE HOUSE STREAM <3 <3 <3

Ozma, a girl with bleached blond hair, is wearing an oversized purple sweatshirt and silver glitter eyeshadow that catches the light when she blinks. Her headset is purple, too.

We can't see much of the room behind her, just the edge of a bed with a stuffed shark sitting on it and a wall decorated with art prints—a pixel-art garden, the Emerald City with a rainbow arcing overhead, several characters from *Sailor Moon*.

Chat

[13:57]—ozma you are seriously so pretty i wish i could be u

In the game she is playing, a house is cross-sectioned so we can see inside. The wallpaper is floral, the furniture a mix of Victorian and modern. Every room is crowded with hanging plants and bright rugs.

In the house, little digital people go about their little digital lives. One is making a sandwich. One is sitting at a computer, staring at the screen.

"Oh dang, Gerald's social is super low."

She selects a menu—a directory of other little digital people, their friendship levels expressed by percentages.

"Okay, who should we invite over? He hasn't really made any friends yet."

[14:20]—me irl lol

"Oh, wait a second, chat. I'm actually getting a call. One moment."

She types something.

"Huh, okay. Well, it's a call from my dear friend Kenneth."

Ozma glances at the camera, raises her eyebrows.

"Hey, hey. I'm live! You're live, Kenneth. This is *Kenneth*, everyone."

The person on the call coughs. When they speak, they are clearly pitching their voice lower than normal.

"Oh, um, hi?"

Ozma adopts a slightly arch tone, bats her eyelashes. The glitter sparkles.

"I'm ever so glad to hear from you, Kenneth. I know how busy your schedule as an investment banker at a major downtown bank can be, dearest Kenneth."

[15:12]—who tf is Kenneth?

A small, tight laugh from the other end of the call.

"Kenneth and I go way back. We met attending one of Canada's top business schools, where we got excellent grades. So, Kenneth, how's business?"

"Not great right now, actually. Um, I'm sorry to interrupt. It's just. There's . . . there's someone outside my, uh, outside my office window. A stranger."

Ozma drops the breezy tone. She sounds serious, now.

"Wait, really? What's going on? Are you okay? Should I stop streaming?"

"Yes, I'm sorry. It's just. I don't know. It's freaking me out. I'm so sorry."

"No, it's fine. It's fine. Are they still there? What are they doing?"

[16:07]—is that Replay? Isn't she banned?

"They're just staring. From the alleyway. Maybe it's nothing. I don't know. But I've been getting a lot of messages lately. From strangers. Like hate messages. Death threats."

[16:58]—shh no this is Kenneth duh

"Aw, shit, yeah. I get those all the time."

"Oh god, you do?"

"Yeah. So does RnBw. They maybe even get more than I do, because at least I don't have to deal with racist shit. You've got to just ignore it, I guess, but it's hard. People get so mad at me for no reason. For just existing."

"I'm so sorry, Ozma."

Ozma shakes her head.

"Like, on the one hand, fuck them. But honestly, part of how I deal with it is to feel pity for those people. They must have such small and bitter lives. Like, thank god I'm not that full of hate all the time. It must eat them from the inside."

[18:00]—Ozma omg you are so inspiring

"Okay, wait, they're moving. Um, they're—I think they're leaving, actually."

"They are? That's great."

Ozma turns her attention briefly back to the game, zooms around to check on each of the little people in the cross-sectioned house. The one at the computer is still just sitting there, staring. Ozma cancels his current task, directs him to go to the kitchen.

"They . . . they had a dog after all. I didn't see it. It was off leash. I feel so silly now. They were just walking a dog. One of those little rat ones. I'm so sorry. I was just being paranoid. Please go back to your stream."

"It's okay, Ken. Don't worry about it. We'll talk later."

[18:42]—we stan Kenneth
[18:43]—Business king

"Yeah. Thank you. Thanks for talking to me."

The call ends. The little dude at the computer hasn't moved yet. He's frozen, motionless.

"Oh, jeez, we should rename him Brick, huh, chat?"

[19:01]—lmao he is us

Ozma cancels all his commands, sends him to the kitchen again. The little guy gets up. He crosses the room, reaches out, turns the doorknob.

[19:07]—open the door

The little guy glitches out, his torso folding in on itself. One of his arms clips through the wall. The other twists back at an unnatural angle.

"Um, you okay there, buddy?"

Then he resets. The door is closed. The animation repeats. He reaches out, turns the doorknob. The pixelated features of his face smear into a blur. He opens the door.

Glitch. Repeat.

His face is gone now. An empty space. Blank.

He opens the door.

He opens the door.

 Hedgelord is live now with 17K viewers
Category: Just Chatting
EXPLORING ABANDONED OFFICE BUILDING

A young white man in a green tracksuit sits cross-legged on the gray-beige carpet of an aggressively bland room.

The walls are blank aside from a few outlets and vents. A mound of trash is piled in one corner—wadded papers, broken particle board, unidentifiable hunks of plastic. The room is dim, but not dark. There's an open doorway leading into another identical room.

Chat

[16:07]—we in the backrooms
[16:07]—omegalul
[16:07]—mild lol

The young man, Hedgelord, stares at the camera, face framed by long strands of blond hair, bleached nearly white. He has a sort of greasy look about him. There are smudges of dust on his tracksuit.

The camera is about five feet away from him, propped on a cardboard box. You can just see the edge of the box at the bottom of the screen.

[16:08]—HEDGE HEDGE HEDGE

[16:08]—u ok bro?

He stares.

[16:09]—sadge

Doesn't move.

[16:09]—he stole brick's look

We've seen this before.

We know what to expect. Hours and hours of silent staring.

[16:10]—this is boring
[16:10]—zZZZzz

But suddenly, Hedge slumps down, arms going loose, head hanging, lank hair falling in a curtain over his face.

[16:11]—WUT
[16:11]—FeelsBadMan
[16:12]—???

Silence.

[16:12]—F
[16:13]—NotLikeThis

[16:14]—naptime

Stillness.

[16:15]—ResidentSleeper
[16:15]—ResidentSleeper
[16:16]—wtf
[16:16]—hedge is dedge
[16:16]—omegalul

And then he gasps, explodes upward in a rush of movement. He lunges at the camera. Tongue out, eyes wide. Screaming.

"Rahhhhhhhh!"

[16:17]—D: D: D:
[16:17]—WAYTOODANK

His shout turns into a laugh. Almost a cackle.

He picks up the camera from the floor and holds it out at arm's length. He is animated, now. Grinning.

"Just fucking with you."

[16:28]—I peed
[16:28]—got me
[16:29]—chat we've been played

[16:29]—knew it
[16:30]—Gigachad move

He's walking now, the camera bobbing along with him.

"I got you, didn't I? I got all of you. Bet you were all like—"

He makes his voice high and mocking.

"Oh no, my favorite streamer is dead. Whatever will I do? Who will I give my millions of dollars to now?"

[16:41]—didn't fool me
[16:41]—yeah right

In the corner opposite the pile of rubble, we see a backpack with some cords sticking out of it. Hedge's mobile-streaming equipment. He hefts it onto his back.

"Well, good news. I'm still here, still ready to receive your primes."

[16:49]—gaslit!

"Or who knows. Maybe you're disappointed. Maybe that's what you want, what you're all secretly hoping for every time you tune into this channel."

[16:56]—hoping for feet pic obvs

He picks up something else from the floor. A bottle of dark liquid. Cola? Whiskey? We can't tell. He takes a swig, shakes his head like it stings, turns back to the camera.

[17:02]—give us a sip of that, hedge

"How about it, chat? You want to see me break down? You want to see me die? Ultimate fail? You'd eat that up, wouldn't you, chat."

[17:12]—lol
[17:13]—no way we love you hedge
[17:13]—wait so that was all fake?

He tucks the bottle into a side pocket of the backpack, pulls out his phone, scrolls through chat with a thumb.

"Yes, chat, I was just messing with you. Brick is faking, too, you know."

He walks across the room, camera still pointed at his face, face pointed at his phone.

[17:22]—copycat

[17:22]—brick is washed up
[17:23]—prove it

"Prove it? Just look at the views he's pulling in with this mad stunt. Respect. He's committed to the bit. I hope he can keep it up. I could only handle like ten minutes before my left ass cheek fell asleep."

[17:36]—omegalul
[17:36]—F for left cheek
[17:36]—open the door

Hedge lopes through the open doorway into the next room, taking us with him. The camera shakes and blurs as he walks.

[17:51]—jfc get a tripod
[17:53]—giving me motion sickness

"Whatever, chat. Let's go explore. This place used to be an office building. I've been eyeing it for a while. It's probably haunted by a thousand office workers whose souls were crushed by the fucking monotony."

[17:57]—I would love a boring office job
[17:57]—heck yes free photocopy

He turns the camera around to face the room, does a slow spin.

"Check this shit out."

This room is nearly identical to the first, except the walls are heavily graffitied, and there's a closed metal door at one end. He crosses the room. We see Hedge's hand reach forward into frame, trying the handle of the door.

[18:19]—did he break in do you think
[18:19]—probably
[18:20]—open the door

It's unlocked. He pushes it open.

We are in a stairwell now. Tall and narrow, it stretches up above to a dirty skylight, and down into darkness.

"What was that?"

The camera view whips around fast, pointing back at the room we just came from. Something darts out of view in the opposite doorway.

"Did you see that, chat? Is there someone else in here?"

[18:30]—huh

[18:31]—I saw it
[18:31]—looked like a person
[18:31]—don't fall for it chat he's
trying to trick us again

"If that's a fucking stream sniper, I'll . . . well, I can't say what I'll do for the sake of TOS. But leave me the fuck alone. How would anyone have found me that fast?"

The camera holds on the doorway for a long moment.

Nothing there. Just the empty doorway.

Shades of beige and gray. Flat shadows. Pockmarked drop ceiling tiles.

Then the camera jerks away.

"Shit."

[18:51]—what was it
[18:52]—i didn't see
[18:52]—a shadow
[18:52]—a person

The view turns back to the stairwell, bobbing as Hedge goes up the stairs, fast. He's running. We can hear him breathing heavily.

[19:01]—lol run hedge run

He reaches the next landing, stops beside another metal door.

"This place is weird, chat."

He sounds out of breath. We see his hand reaching out again, pushing open a second metal door.

[19:13]—open the door

We can see into the room now. Another abandoned office. This one still has a few desks. And the overhead fluorescent lights are on, flickering.

In the middle of the room: an office chair with a crooked backrest.

It is spinning gently. As if someone had just nudged it.

[19:24]—oh damn

Hedge takes a step back from the door, the camera moving with him.

[19:30]—so cursed

Another step back.

Another step.

The light in the room flickers off.

> [19:36]—aw hell nah
> [19:36]—get out of there
> [19:36]—WAY TOO DANK

The camera suddenly jolts upward, the wall smearing past us. A glimpse of the stairs continuing upward. The skylight far above.

> [19:37]—shit

And then shaking and juddering. Clanging. Everything is blurring and shaking.

Disjointed flashes of light and dark.

This all only lasts a second. Maybe two.

A crunch. The camera goes dark.

> [19:38]—what's happening

He's fallen.

He's fallen backward over the railing of the stairwell.

The connection holds on for another second, lines of digital noise cutting into the darkness, bright jagged shards.

[19:38]—D:

The stream ends.

11://

Teresa watches Hedge run. She watches him fall.

And when it's over?

She posts the clip.

She doesn't feel bad about it. He was faking the whole thing. He admitted it. He probably just threw the camera at the end. It seems like the sort of thing he would do. He's known for streaming in public places, pulling pranks, pushing the boundaries of what's allowed on the platform. He was always getting kicked out of stores or restaurants. He's streamed from a rollercoaster, an airplane, the DMV, a casino.

It's making Teresa doubt the whole thing. Hedge said Brick was faking and sure, most people online think the same thing, but Hedge actually knows Brick. It's possible they've talked.

So what if it is just a big joke? What if they're all in on it, all pretending?

Teresa's paranoia had her convinced that the dogwalker in the alleyway was an internet stalker coming to kill her. Maybe she can't trust herself anymore. Can't trust her own eyes, her own mind. Maybe she fell for the trick hard because she's off the deep end.

Her brother was right about one thing. She *has* been getting worse.

She hasn't showered in four days now. She'd been venturing to the bathroom less and less, but as of last night, she can't go there at all and so she has had to resort to using an empty water bottle. She's hidden it in a corner, but the shame is hot and bright.

If she doesn't find a way to stop this, her world will shrink and shrink the way it has been shrinking ever since the accident, contracting around her until it is too small to contain her body. Until there is no safe place anywhere.

She checks the streams. Horsegirl and KingCoal are still staring in silence. No change there, except that their chats are now flooded with accusations that they are faking like Hedge. Brick is still speaking sporadically, spitting out weird snippets that seem to be mostly copied from the chat.

Teresa skims back over the document where she's been compiling screencaps and transcripts as evidence. She sees the follow list for the user Tjbnfskha. Maybe that account really is just an alt of Brick's. He has at least one alt account—Bricktwo—which he streams from when he wants to be more casual. More real.

If Brick is not truly in danger, then there's absolutely no justification for Replay's last stream. She shouldn't have doxxed him either way, of course, she can see that now, but at the time she genuinely thought she was helping.

Maybe she really does need to make an apology video.

She sets up her camera. Her hair is a mess, but she forges ahead. "Hey, everyone," she starts, and then shakes her head. Too chipper, too cheerful. She'll edit it out. She tries again. "We need to talk about Brick."

That could work as a title. She can picture the thumbnail. A shot of Brick with her own face superimposed to the side, looking apologetic.

If he really is faking, though, shouldn't he be sorry, too? He's taking it too far. He's scaring people. Giving impressionable fans dangerous delusions. Giving them hallucinations.

Her eyes dart to her door. It is open a crack, the way she left it.

She turns her camera off. She can't focus. Something is nagging at her.

She rewatches the clip she posted from the end of Hedge's stream. She slows it down, goes through frame by frame. Mostly, it is incomprehensible. Blurs and smudges of color and light.

But there, you can see an arm flailing for an instant. A few frames later, a leg.

Was that part real?

She goes back to the raw recorded footage, finds the moment before Hedge turned and ran. The camera is pointed away from him, toward an empty doorway. She clicks through frame by frame.

Empty doorway. Empty doorway. Empty doorway. And then just for an instant, the figure appears. The shadow. Just the way it looked on Brick's stream and on Replay's stream.

She can feel panic fizzing up inside of her. She doesn't know what to believe anymore, what to think. She's so alone, cut off from everyone.

At least there's Ozma. Her one shining star. Teresa will explain everything to her when they talk later. Ozma's good at giving reality checks. She can help Teresa figure this out.

She wishes they could talk now, but Ozma is probably still live.

Teresa checks Ozma's stream.

She refreshes.

Refreshes again.

No.

There's no way.

She refreshes and refreshes, but it's not a glitch. The stream isn't frozen.

Ozma is.

Her beautiful, funny friend isn't playing the game, isn't smiling, isn't cracking a quick-witted joke. She's just sitting there, expression dull and slack, staring straight ahead.

She wouldn't fake it.

Teresa is sure of that.

And it's here now, slamming into her, the panic attack. It is overflowing, flooding every sense. Teresa wants to run, wants to escape, but there is nowhere to go, no way to escape.

She can't breathe. Her chest is tight. Is it a heart attack, actually? Every time she has a panic attack, she thinks it might be a heart attack and it never is a heart attack, but maybe this is the exception. The one time.

Teresa unpeels from herself. Her mind goes floating up and up, a helium balloon let go by a careless child except the careless child is her own body.

It doesn't calm her down, exactly, but it helps a little. The panic feels more distant. Nothing feels quite real. The world has taken on a fake, plastic quality. If nothing is real, nothing can hurt her. Teresa moves. Her body feels like a clunky robot she is piloting, poorly, from afar.

She grabs her phone. She calls Ozma, though she knows it is probably useless. The phone rings and rings.

What does she do? What *can* she do, stuck here in her room, helpless and powerless and so, so alone? She paces in a tight circle, calling Ozma over and over, listening to the endless ringing. No answer. No way to reach her. Ozma is trapped, like the princess in the movie. Not in a mirror, but on a screen.

Ozma lives in West Virginia, the next state over. Teresa has the address. She runs over to her closet, fumbles through a pile of clothes and papers until she finds the envelope from Ozma. She'd sent Teresa a bunch of stickers just last month, all handpicked to her interests. Rainbows. Pixel art. Potted plants. Several are stuck to the back of her phone case now. Teresa types in Ozma's return address. It's only an hour and forty-five minutes away from here.

Only?

It could be five minutes away and Teresa still couldn't go there.

She returns to pacing. She needs to figure this out, figure out how to stop it. She checks her messages, which are flooding in faster than she can keep up with, and finds a reply from another commenter on the forum post about Kyle's death. This person said they were from the same town as Kyle. Teresa had messaged to ask them for more information.

> [−] from Big_julio568739
>
> So what I heard is it was basically a combination of stimulants that got him. He was stacking caffeine pills, energy drinks, and adderall so he could stream all night after working his day job. Maybe even regular old speed, too, I don't know. But it basically fried his system. He had a seizure and his heart gave out. Kind of sad.

Very sad, if that's true, but it doesn't help her. It doesn't explain anything about what's happening now.

Another new message snags her attention.

Tjbnfskha
hello

She stares at it for a long moment, heart racing. How silly to be afraid of a nonsense word. But she is afraid of everything she can't understand—death, flirting, why bad things happen to good people—and she doesn't understand this.

She types a response, hits send.

who is this?

The reply comes back immediately.

I think you know

 Brick is live now with 8.4K viewers
Category: Just Chatting
OPEN THE DOOR

Brick's eyes are so bloodshot that they are nearly more red than white. He has a manic glint. Individual beads of sweat stand out on his forehead, catching tiny reflections of the screen.

"Let's go."

> **Chat**
>
> [30:08:22]—lets go!
> [30:08:23]—I'm here for the long haul
> [30:08:23]—brought the popcorn

He's been talking more.

Moving, even. Isolated, jerky gestures.

"Do it."

> [30:08:25]—do wat bro?
> [30:08:25]—these r clues
> [30:08:26]—has anyone been keeping track of everything he says?

His eyes dart around wildly sometimes, as if he's looking for something.

"Open the door."

> [30:08:28]—yeah there's a google doc
> [30:08:28]—check the fan server
> [30:08:29]—open the door

His speech, like his movement, is in brief, staccato bursts.

"I love you."

> [30:08:33]—lololol he luvs us
> [30:08:34]—<3 <# <3
> [30:08:34]—aw we love you too brick
> [30:08:35]—open the door

His voice has grown in intensity over the last few hours. It is no longer a whisper.

"Look."

> [30:08:36]—we r looking
> [30:08:36]—open the door
> [30:08:37]—look at what?

There's still something off about it, though.

"Follow me."

> [30:08:38]—followin already
> [30:08:39]—y is he talking so weird
> [30:08:40]—is this supposed to make sense

He doesn't move his lips as much as he should. Sometimes the consonants are too soft, lost and inaudible.

"Say that."

> [30:08:41]—what does he want us to say?
> [30:08:41]—open the door i think

It grows more obvious as he gets louder, this sense of the words being forced out.

"Just read this one little thing."

> [30:08:45]—sure why not
> [30:08:46]—open the door

Air blown through a tube in the shape of a man.

"Open the door."

> [30:08:50]—open the door
> [30:08:51]—open the door

He is getting faster. Getting louder.

"Chat."

> [30:08:55]—yes?
> [30:08:55]—open the door
> [30:08:55]—open the door
> [30:08:55]—open the door
> [30:08:56]—open the door

And then all of a sudden he is talking in a mad rush, the words no longer isolated but all jammed together, stumbling over each other.

> "Everyone do it open the door open the door to
> real just this one little thing you follow me I used
> to follow open the door big fan my heart let it fly
> open the door open the door say that open the
> door open the door open the door let's go we
> can do it thank you all you need to do open the
> door thanks I love you open the open the door I
> love you I love you open the—"

As suddenly as it started, it ends.

Brick slumps over, body limp. His head hits the desk with a loud crack. The keyboard jumps under the impact.

[30:09:18]—open the door
[30:09:18]—open the door
[30:09:18]—open the door
[30:09:19]—open t

12://

Teresa isn't watching Brick. She's not watching any of them. She's staring at her phone, at the message she just got.

> who is this?

> **Tjbnfskha**
> I think you know

She definitely does not know. She types "leave me alone" and then deletes it. If this person has any useful information, she's got to find out.

> what's going on?

> what do you have to do with all this?

> You haven't figured it out yet?

> I'm surprised

> I thought you were smart

> are you even a real person?

> I'm real

Maybe this is just a troll. Some random guy getting off on freaking out strangers. Maybe it's a coincidence that the same screen name showed up when Kyle died, and right before things got weird with Brick, and in her DMs.

Thump.

Teresa jumps, the sound like a match to the dry kindling of her pulse. Her heart bursts into flame. It's not her door this time. The sound came from down the hall.

It was a strange *thump*, heavy and loud. She felt it, too, through the floor.

"Jason?" she calls, but in a voice too quiet to do any good.

She thinks of the figure she saw in the alleyway. She was so quick to dismiss the whole thing when she saw they had a dog, but that could have been a cover, right? What if it had been an internet stalker after all?

Images flash through her mind, like a video compilation that she can't pause, can't turn off. Someone climbing up the side of the house, crawling through a window, creeping through the hallway. A knife. A gun. A strangling rope.

She creeps softly to her bedroom door. She listens for more *thump*s, for footfalls. Some confirmation of her fears.

Only silence.

She waits for what feels like an agonizingly long time, listening, bracing herself, but all she hears is her own heartbeat.

"Jason?" she shouts louder this time. "Jason!"

Her parents are out. It's just the two of them alone in the house. Maybe Jason is messing with her, or he's got headphones on. She tries calling him on her phone. Would he even pick up if he saw her name? Or does he hate her too much?

Well, he isn't picking up.

She tries again.

A third time.

Her mind is playing a new compilation now. Her brother crushed beneath a fallen bookcase. Her brother bleeding out. Her brother concussed, unconscious. Alone on the floor of his room.

"Jason!" she shouts, loud as she can.

There is no answer, but still she hesitates.

She can't go out there.

She can't she can't she can't.

He could just be ignoring her. He could be messing with her on purpose.

But what if she does nothing? What if she does nothing and he dies? What if this is like that night with Becks all over again? She can't let that happen.

All the conflicting voices in her mind are drowned out, finally, by the churning rush of her fear. A frothing river of pure adrenaline that carries her, that makes her body move faster than her mind.

The door isn't all the way closed, so she can only hope it doesn't count as opening it when she shoves her foot in the gap and kicks it just wide enough to slide through. She lunges out into the hallway, stumbles the short distance between her room and her brother's room.

Another compilation is playing in her head now, but this one is real.

This one is a memory.

A narrow road with no shoulders, twisting through the forested hills. A night so dark she could see nothing except a narrow slice of road illuminated by headlights. It felt as if the rest of the world had been erased, as if the only thing left was her and Becks, the car, that sliver of road.

They were singing together, laughing. Free. As close to careless as Teresa had ever been in her life.

And then a flash of something white on the road up ahead.

A deer?

The car lurched to the side. She'd turned the wheel too fast, too violently. Her fault. All her fault. A wall of trees sprang up ahead of her.

Teresa doesn't remember the impact. Doesn't remember how it sounded, how it felt.

She just remembers the stunned silence afterward. Her ears ringing, view obscured by what she thought was smoke at first but realized later, when it settled like snow on the car's surfaces, was powder from the airbag. She coughed. Something dripped from her nose. The pain registered on a slight delay. Her head ached. Angry red friction burns screamed from her forearms.

She turned and there was Becks, slumped over, held up by her seat belt. Teresa reached over and grabbed her arm, dug her fingers in hard. *Becks? Becks!*

"Jason!"

His door is partway open. She kicks it the rest of the way, barges in.

No blood, no guts, no broken window, no fallen shelf, no agonized death throes. She takes that in quickly, measuring the quiet room against the worst-case scenarios her mind had conjured so vividly.

Her little brother is simply sitting on the floor in front of his desk. His chair has rolled back to the opposite wall, as if he slid right out of it. That must have been the *thump*.

"Jason?"

He doesn't react.

"Jason?"

She runs to him. His legs are splayed out, his arms hang loose at his sides. His eyes are open, but he isn't moving.

"Jason, stop it. You're scaring me. Stop it."

She pinches his arm, but he doesn't move, doesn't react. She doesn't want to jostle him too much, doesn't want to shake him, just in case.

Is he breathing? Oh god. She holds her hand in front of his face, feels the slightest tickle as he exhales.

He's alive. But what's wrong with him?

She pulls her phone out of her pocket, frantically searches: "My brother isnt moving."

My brother isnt moving.   X

Did you mean: my brother *isn't* moving.

● Quora

My brother is twenty-eight and won't move out of our parent's house and has never had a job. How can I encourage him to . . .

● Reddit

AITA for telling my brother I'm not moving back home even if : . .

People also ask:

What to do if a sibling is distant?

She tries again. "Unresponsive person." "Sudden coma out of nowhere." "How do you make someone wake up if their eyes are open." The internet says to place the person in the recovery position. The internet says to wait for help to arrive. It says people also ask, "What is the difference between unresponsive and dead."

This isn't helping.

She tries calling her parents, but there's no answer. Their phones must be on silent for the performance. She sends them a text anyway: *pls come home right away*. Maybe they'll see it at intermission, but then again, it's been a long time since she truly believed her parents could keep her safe. She misses that childhood certainty, when it seemed like her parents could fix any problem. There's no one to turn to anymore, no one to protect her. She's got to fix this herself.

She waves her hands back and forth in front of Jason's face. He doesn't track her hand, doesn't seem to see. He's just staring straight ahead at the mess of cords beneath his desk.

Before he fell, he would have been staring at his computer.

Teresa looks up at Jason's screen for the first time, notices what is on there. What is still playing. What Jason must have been watching.

Brick's stream.

She stands up, leaning close to the screen. She hadn't seen it happen live, the moment when Brick collapsed. She feels a tiny pang of regret.

It would have made a good clip.

She shakes her head, as if to dislodge the thought. Is she a bad person for even thinking that? She peers closer, at the small slumped-over figure.

Is *Brick* breathing? Is he moving? He probably just passed out from exhaustion, right?

The chat isn't moving either, which is weird. Usually on Brick's streams, the words race down the side of the screen so fast she can barely read them, but now as she watches, only one message comes through. There are still over eight thousand people watching, though, according to the view counter.

She should turn the stream off, focus on her brother.

But something is happening now, on the stream. Something awful. She can't look away.

 Brick is live now with 8.4K viewers
Category: Just Chatting
OPEN THE DOOR

Brick has not moved since he first collapsed face down onto his desk. Not so much as a tremor.

Chat

[30:13:47]—i missed it what happened
[30:13:54]—hello? anyone else here?
[30:14:01]—it says there are like ten thousand of you watching why is no one talking?

Knocking in the distance.

[30:14:05]—hey i just tuned in
[30:14:10]—did he pass out?

A *bang*.

[30:14:21]—im not sure whats going on

Another *bang*. Something falling. Footsteps. Barely audible voices.

"All clear in here."

More footsteps. A knock on the door. A voice from the hallway, louder now.

"Open up! Police!"

[30:14:55]—oh damn

The door slams open. We can see two men in the hallway. Cops. Black uniforms, bulky belts strapped with weapons.

[30:14:56]—did someone swat him?

The two men shout. Clipped declaratives. Harsh and blunt.

"Don't move."

He's not moving.

"Hands up."

He's not doing that either.

"Down on the ground."

They repeat the same phrases over and over, getting louder each time, the words overlapping and blurring into one another.

One of the cops pulls his gun from his belt.

[30:15:16]—this isn't going to end well

The first cop takes a step into the room. He sweeps it with his gun, as though the gun is the one taking a look.

"Oh shit, there's another one."

The second cop steps into the room, speaks into a walkie-talkie on his chest.

"We're going to need an ambulance."

The first cop goes out of frame. The second walks toward Brick, toward us.

[30:15:37]—HEY PIG
[30:15:39]—Omg don't say that

"Sir? Sir?"

He puts one hand on Brick's shoulder. The other hovers at the gun on his belt.

Brick doesn't move. The cop shakes his shoulder roughly. Brick's arm flops limply.

"I don't think he's breathing."

The other cop responds from off-screen.

"No pulse on this one."

"Shit. Narcan?"

"Let the EMTs handle it."

The second cop puts two fingers to Brick's neck. Shakes his head.

[30:16:07]—this can't be happening

There's a crackle of static from his walkie-talkie. A stream of words barely audible. Something that might be "on the way." The cop turns his attention to the computer.

"His camera is still on, I think."

"Turn it off."

The cop's hands come right at us. He is fumbling at the webcam mounting, his hands blocking the view. The first cop shouts at him, moving back into frame.

"I said turn it off."

"I'm trying."

[30:16:22]—fuck the police for real tho

The camera tilts. We catch a glimpse of something on the floor.

A hand. An arm.

A woman lies on the floor, her eyes open, staring at nothing.

Lil.

The camera tilts back. We see the two cops again. The second one is leaning over Brick, squinting at the monitor, trying to click something. The first hovers behind him.

[30:16:58]—did anybody clip that??

"Is it off?"

"I told you I'm trying."

"Just shut the whole thing down."

Something moves in the open doorway. The second cop sees it on the monitor. He jumps back, his gun drawn in an instant. He points it at the doorway.

At the shadowy figure.

[30:17:09]—omg

"What the hell are you doing?"

The first cop has turned toward the doorway, but he can't see it. Of course he can't.

"Someone was there. Just a second ago. There's someone else in the house."

"Jesus fucking Christ, man. Cool it. There's no one there."

"I saw someone. I swear I did, just now. On the screen."

The shadow figure takes a step forward.

"Did you turn it off?"

"No, but . . ."

"Oh, for fuck's sake."

The first cop reaches for the camera. He rips it off its mounting.

The second cop is shouting.

"Show yourself! Police! Come out with your hands up!"

We can't see anything now. The camera has fallen to the desk, landed on its back, pointing up at the ceiling. There's a faint water stain there, in the corner.

[30:17:36]—this isn't happening

The stream finally ends.

OFFLINE

Brick is offline.

🔔 You will be notified when Brick is live

Thanks for tuning in, see you soon!

Join the official server
follow @Brick

13://

Teresa watches, rapt with horror. Lil can't be dead. Brick can't be dead. They can't be. An ambulance was coming, wasn't it? The cops must have been wrong. Brick and Lil will both be alive. They'll both be fine. They'll sit up and smile, say *just kidding*.

The moment the stream ends, Teresa catches movement out of the corner of her eye. Her brother.

"Jason?"

She kneels beside him again. Snaps her fingers in his face. Begs him to wake up. Threatens to post his most embarrassing baby photos online for all his classmates to see. He doesn't react to any of it.

There's something odd about his eyes. She peers close, face uncomfortably close to his. He'd yell at her if he wasn't unresponsive.

His pupils are wide, dilated.

And they each reflect a perfect rectangle of light.

There's nothing in front of him. No light.

Well, except the computer screen. The angle seems wrong since it's up on the desk and he's on the floor, but that must be it. She jumps to her feet again, scrabbling for the mouse. She shuts the whole thing down. It goes too slow, nagging her with pop-ups about open programs, which she clicks away furiously.

And then finally the computer whirs once, like heaving a sigh of relief, and the screen blips to black.

Jason jerks again. His arm twitches. She is by his side in an instant.

"Jason? Jason?"

He doesn't move again. Reflected in his eyes, though there is no possible source now: the little glowing rectangles.

She tries one more frantic search on her phone: "Can the internet kill you?"

What is she hoping for? Proof that she's wrong about her theory? Some kind of reassurance that everything is going to be okay?

All she gets is op-eds about social media rotting our brains and conspiracy posts from people who claim to be sensitive to electromagnetic fields. These people are constructing Faraday cages in their living rooms. They are moving in droves to a small town in the center of a thirteen-thousand-square-mile region designated the National Radio Quiet Zone. It's only a few hours away—in West Virginia, the same state where Ozma lives—but Teresa has never heard of it.

She reads for a few moments longer than she meant to, momentarily distracted. Wi-Fi and cellphone use are strictly limited there so as not to interfere with the delicate readings taken by nearby telescopes. The telescopes have captured images of supermassive black holes. They are part of the SETI program, searching for extraterrestrial life.

Teresa never really believed in aliens. She never believed in demons or ghosts or any of that nonsense before now.

She opens her messages, types a question.

> are you doing this?

The answer comes lightning-fast, as if the person on the other end had just been watching their phone this whole time, waiting for her.

> **Tjbnfskha**
> You already know the answer to that
>
> don't you?

Teresa thinks maybe she does. She thinks whoever—whatever—she is speaking to now is the answer to all this. The one behind it.

The shadow figure.

A demon. Or a ghost. It killed Kyle and then found its way to Brick and killed him and now it has found its way here. To her own house. Her own little brother.

Is that her fault? Did she lead the ghost here somehow? Invite it in?

> please stop
>
> leave Jason alone

> who?

Maybe she shouldn't be having this conversation. Maybe it is foolish, dangerous. But she's got to do something. She's got to at least try.

> why are you talking to me?
>
> what do you want?

> you're not like the others

what?

you've been helping me

She hasn't been helping them. She's trying to stop them. What do they mean?

She is halfway through typing that question when the answer hits her. She posted that clip of the shadowy figure appearing on Brick's stream. She spread their image, far and wide. Spread their message. *Open the door.* She has posted so many more clips since then, too. Every time they appeared. She helped give them a bigger audience. A captive audience.

Is this really her fault? Is all of it her fault? Ozma and Jason and Lil and Brick. And Becks. It can't be her fault. Not again.

what did you do to Brick?

did you kill him?

Brick . . .

I used to be a big fan, you know

I used to think he cared about his community

but now I think he is just feeding off us

Teresa blinks down at her phone. She's seen those words before. Those exact words. In a forum post from a year ago. She tries one more time.

who are you?

you tell me

. . . Kyle?

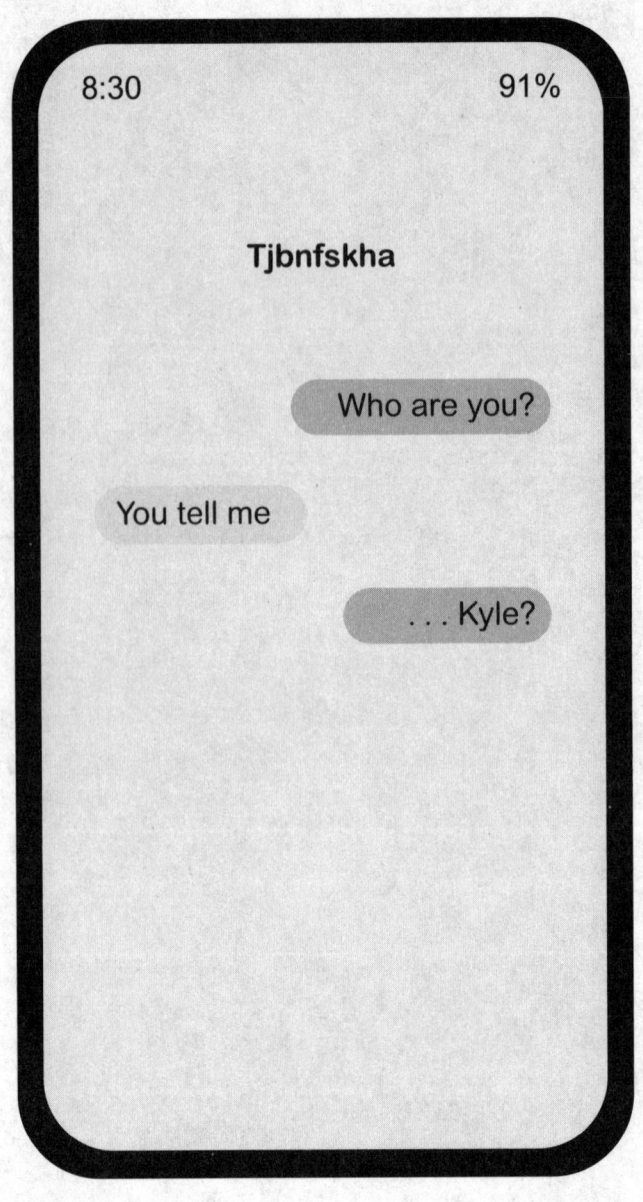

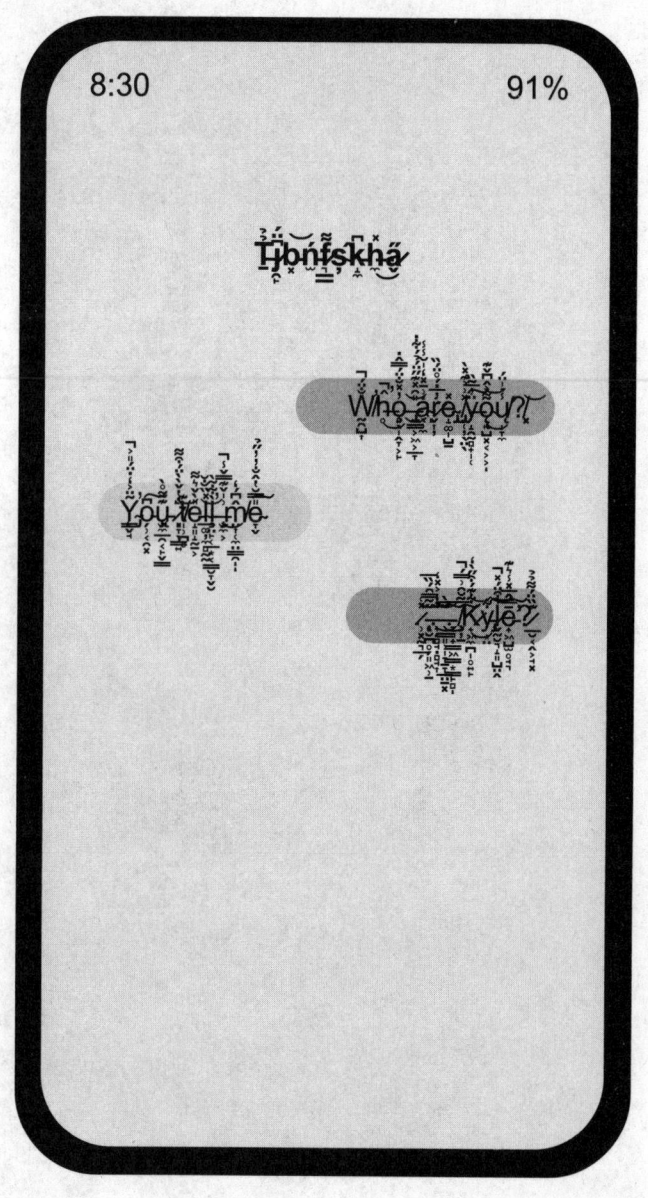

8:30 91%

Ḷḅnískh̃ǎ

Who are you?

You tell me

Kyle?

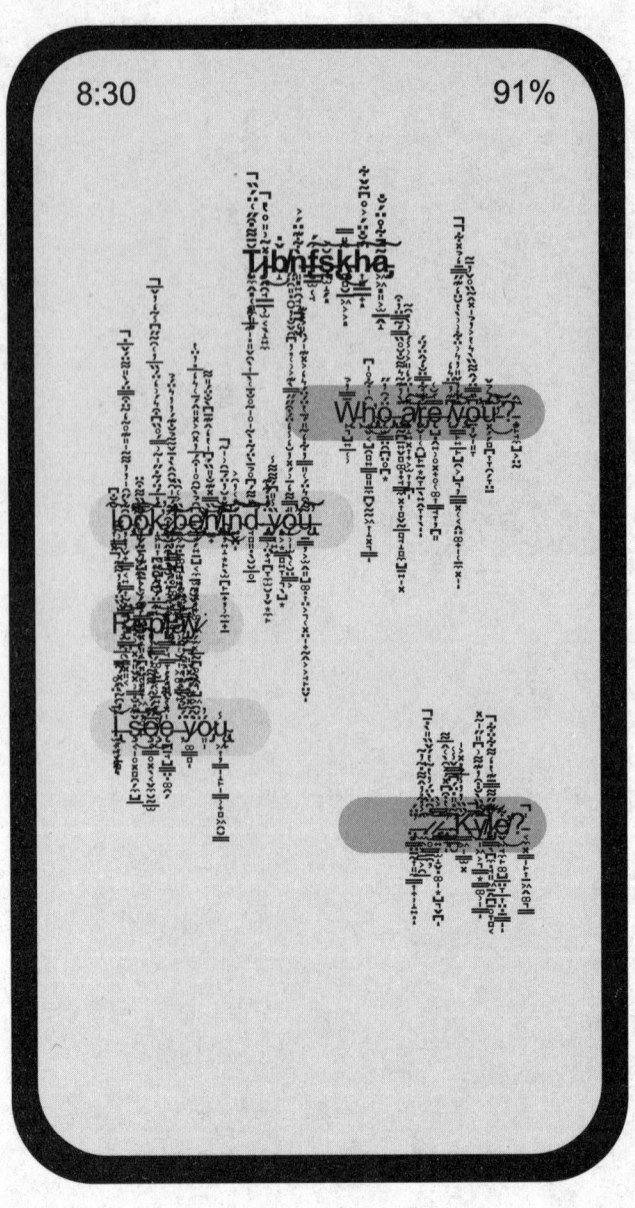

14://

Teresa drops her phone. It's got an expensive clear case, so it doesn't break. The screen doesn't shatter. It doesn't even crack.

It just sits there on the floor, face up. Staring at her. She thinks she understands now.

The ghost didn't kill Kyle.

The ghost *is* Kyle.

The solitary user watching him when he died was no demon, no murderer. The truth is simpler and sadder. Tjbnfskha wasn't Brick's alt account. It was Kyle's. He was watching himself stream, artificially boosting his views. It's technically against the rules to do that, but she's heard about people trying.

She grabs her phone, holds the power button down until it shuts off, the smiley face giving way to slick black nothing. She can see her own reflection in the screen—an indistinct outline. A shadow. Like the figure on the streams.

Ghosts haunt the place they died, don't they? Kyle died while he was streaming, he died while he was live.

Teresa laughs, a little hysterically. You can't be *live* when you're dead, can you?

She runs back to her room and yanks the power cord to her computer. Shuts down her laptop.

The internet makes dead things live on. Dead memes. Dead people. Kyle's main streaming account had been deleted, but the video of his death is still out there, and so is his alt account. No one had known about it, probably. No one had bothered to delete it after he died. Somehow, he's found a way to remain. He's haunting the alt account. Or maybe just haunting the internet itself.

So does that mean ghosts are real? Does that mean people can live on after death? Does that mean Becks could have . . .

But Teresa can't let herself think about that. Not now.

Back down the hall. Jason's room. She touches his shoulder, says his name, tries not to break down. He still isn't moving, but there's more than just their two computers in the house. Her parents have laptops. They have an automated home assistant. They even have a smart fridge. Her father was over the moon for a week when he first bought it. It was basically all he could talk about. *Can you believe this*, he'd say. The fridge could tell when they ran out of milk. It compiled a shopping list for them. *What a miracle. What a world we live in*. He didn't feel the same way about streaming, unfortunately.

This is her fault, isn't it? On her stream, she played the footage of the shadowy figure over and over. On her video channel, she posted the clip of his first appearance. She invited the ghost in. She helped him spread, gave him power, unleashed him on the world. And now he's got Jason and it's all her fault and she's got to fix it, no matter the cost.

Teresa runs.

Runs without thinking. She can't think or she won't be able to do this.

She runs downstairs. She feels like she is floating, like her feet aren't quite touching the stairs, like this is a dream where the rules of gravity are all wrong. A nightmare. Her eyes go instinctively to the front door as she passes it, to the many windows, but the danger is invisible now. It's in the air. It is everywhere. Inescapable.

The lights are off downstairs, and the sun has dipped below the trees outside. The once-familiar shapes of the furniture have grown strange in the dimness, hulking and vague. She flinches at the sight of the television.

She finds the Wi-Fi router, tucked halfway behind the TV stand, betrayed only by a line of little blinking green lights. She yanks the cord from the wall and the lights blink off.

"Jason?" she shouts.

There's no sound from upstairs, so maybe that wasn't enough either. She isn't sure if this will work, but she can't stop and think, or she'll freeze, immobilized by fear. She runs into the kitchen. The basement door is open. She takes a deep breath, heads down.

She tries not to look at the rusty pipes or the cobwebs or the husks of dead insects, tries not to imagine the live ones that might be lurking in the corners. She's had a wretched fear of swarming insects ever since she was a kid, ever since she was six and she dozed off in the backyard while holding a popsicle and woke to find her arm and one leg absolutely encrusted in tiny black ants. She screamed and screamed and kept screaming long after her parents had rushed out and brushed the ants away and carried her back inside.

It is horrible down here in the basement, contaminated and unsafe. The air smells like mold, but she can't let herself stop moving.

She finds the fuse box, throws the breaker, cuts off all electricity to the house. The basement is plunged into darkness. Now she can't see the cobwebs at all, can't see if anything is lurking in the corners, and that's so much worse. Her pulse beats like a drum in her ears. Her fear is a physical presence, hovering just over her shoulder, breathing on her neck as she feels her way back to the stairs in the dark, skids through the kitchen as though something is chasing her, runs up the other stairs, doesn't stop until she is standing once more at her brother's door. She's panting. She hasn't moved that much or that far in weeks.

Jason hasn't moved at all.

He's still just sitting there, legs splayed, staring sightlessly at the cords beneath his desk. Was she wrong? Maybe this has nothing to do with the ghost. Maybe a blood clot broke loose, traveled to his brain.

Or maybe she was just too late.

What if Jason is gone? What if there's no saving him? She can't deal with that. She can't even think about it. Some days she still feels like her grief for Becks is strong enough to kill her. Her guilt. She can't go through that again. If Jason dies and it is her fault. Her fault again. She can't think about it, but she is thinking about it and she can't breathe, she can't—

Her gaze catches on a glint of light from the floor, something reflecting the dim sunset glow from the window.

His phone. Of course.

She scrambles for it, shuts it down.

She is cut off, now. Entirely. Alone in the dark. For a moment she is frozen. Staring down at Jason's phone, though there is nothing to see, thumb hovering over the power button.

And then from behind her, a faint groan.

She spins around.

Jason is still sitting on the floor, but he's rubbing his eyes now, he's moving, he's awake. Teresa's legs go weak with relief, her adrenaline high crashing back down to earth.

"Teresa?" Jason says, squinting at her. She's half-expecting him to be angry at her, to yell at her for being in his room, for turning off his computer, for existing. But he looks confused and scared, and suddenly very young again. "What are you doing here?"

"I . . ." she starts but then stops because she is crying. She's embarrassed, but she can't help it.

"You're out of your room." Jason climbs stiffly to his feet, glances at the displaced desk chair. "What's going on?"

Instead of answering, Teresa lunges forward and hugs him.

"Ugh, get off," he says, but there's no malice in his tone, and when he pushes her away, it's only a gentle shove.

"I thought you were dead," she says through her tears.

"What? That's ridiculous. I mean, I just . . . I just fell asleep." He goes to his computer, jiggles the mouse. Tries to switch on his desk lamp. "Is the power out?"

Teresa wipes her eyes, pulls herself together. "Yeah, I turned it off. But Jason, I don't think you were asleep."

"I must have been." He turns to her, frowning. He looks like someone who has just woken up from sleep, bleary and distant. "I was dreaming."

A shiver runs down Teresa's spine. Jason's window is open. Teresa resists the urge to go over and close it. A thin halo of orange light limns the tops of the trees outside.

"What did you dream about?" she asks.

"Why did you turn the power off?" he asks instead of answering. "Why are you in here?"

"You fell out of your chair." She gestures at it. "I heard it from my room."

"Guess I'm turning into Dad." Their father falls asleep sitting up all the time, head tilted onto the back of the couch, TV still playing. Jason chuckles, but it sounds a bit strained. He's scared but trying to hide it, Teresa can tell.

She's doing the same thing.

"You were watching Brick's stream, right?" she asks.

"Yeah?" he says, as if this might be a trick question. "Weren't you watching it too?"

"No. What happened?"

Jason rolls his desk chair back to its normal place. He slumps down into it, rubs his eyes. "Um, he was shouting a lot? Mostly about doors, but also a bunch of other stuff that made no sense." He shrugs. "And then I fell asleep."

Teresa is thinking about how slow Brick's chat was moving, after he collapsed. What if the ghost found a way to travel through the stream? To get to the people watching. What if there are thousands of people out there right now, catatonic just like Jason had been?

Like Ozma still is, probably.

"You had a dream?" she asks him.

"I guess it was like a nightmare." He seems embarrassed. "It was silly though. Like it wasn't really anything."

"Tell me about it, Jason. Please."

"Fine." He's spinning his chair back and forth gently. When they were kids, they would take turns spinning each other in that chair until they got so dizzy they nearly puked. "It was like I was in this huge cavern or something. It was dark. Too dark to see. But I could tell there was something out there. Getting closer. I couldn't move. I couldn't do anything."

"I don't think it was a dream," says Teresa. "I think you were possessed."

Jason snorts.

"I mean it," she says. "Your eyes were open, Jason."

She sees him flinch, ever so slightly. "Really?"

"Yes. You wouldn't wake up, no matter what. Not until I turned off all the computers and phones and cut the power to the house." Should she tell Jason about her theory? She doesn't think he'll believe her, but she's got to try. She takes a deep breath, forges ahead. "There's this . . . this ghost. I think it's haunting people through the internet somehow. Possessing people. It possessed Brick. That's why he was acting so strange, why he couldn't talk at first. Why he . . . well, I think it's all because the ghost was battling him for control."

Jason is looking at her like she's talking absolute nonsense. Well, that's nothing new. She can deal with that.

"Wait," he says. "You went downstairs?"

She laughs once, short and sharp. It's not really funny. None of this is funny. Out the window, the orange halo has slipped away from the tops of the trees. The sun is almost gone, the sky getting darker by the second. The room is getting darker too.

She pulls her dead phone out of her pocket.

"I'm going to turn this back on," she says to Jason. "And I'll show you what I'm talking about. But you have to promise me that if I freeze up or something, you'll take it and turn it off. Okay? I know you don't believe me, but please just promise me that."

When they were little—or hell, even as recently as two or three years ago—Jason would follow Teresa around like a duckling, trailing her all around the house, the yard, the neighborhood. She'd try to lose him, but he was persistent, unrelenting. It got on her nerves back then, but now she needs him to follow her again, just for a little while.

"Promise," she says again.

"Okay, sure. Whatever." He really does seem scared. Whether he's scared of what happened to him or scared that his sister is having a psychotic break, she isn't sure. But she can't reassure him. She can't tell him everything will be fine. They left fine behind a long time ago.

She presses the power button on her phone. If anything happens, she can just throw her phone, smash it. It's only a little internet, only a little window, surely nothing can climb through. Right?

The dark reflection of her face in the glass gives way to a bright glowing grid of icons. A moment, two, and then the notifications flood in.

Streamer Brick Dies During Bizarre Marathon Stream

By Toni Ewing

February 23, 8:54 p.m. EDT

Nicholas Corey, 23, known by thousands of online fans as Brick, was reported dead earlier today by the Bexar County police department after a <u>possible swatting incident</u> on Corey's stream.

Corey, better known by his online alias "Brick," began streaming as Brick five years ago and had since built himself a significant following across multiple platforms. He was known as a "variety" streamer, rather than being associated with a single game or type of content. His streams occasionally drew viewership in the hundreds of thousands.

On his most recent stream, <u>Corey attracted attention for staring at the camera in silence for many hours</u>, a possible stunt or form of performance art. Approximately thirty hours into the stream, two officers can be seen entering Corey's room with guns drawn.

The <u>official statement</u> provided by the department claims that Corey and one other adult, currently unidentified, were both found already deceased at the time of officers' arrival on the scene. Cause of death is unconfirmed. The department stated that their investigation is ongoing.

It's a difficult day for the streaming community, as this report comes less than an hour after streamer <u>Hedgelord was found dead</u> in an abandoned office building in Florida. Hedgelord was reportedly trespassing at the time of his death. The incident is being treated as an accident.

Spearden County police department did not return our request for further comment.

Updated 8:05 p.m. EDT

Multiple sources now report that viewers of Brick's last stream have become catatonic, possibly a case of social contagion or mass psychogenic illness.

Sign up for our newsletter to get the latest delivered to your inbox

We All Use Our Phones On the Toilet, but Is There a Hidden Cost?	Livestreaming Turned Deadly for Streamer Hedgelord	Top 20 Habits of Most Successful Content Creators

Jolley

Hey what's going on with Ozma?

Have you seen her stream?

Why is she acting like Brick?

Did you two talk about this or something?

Replay???

I'm not mad about it or anything I just

want to know what's going on

and like if everything is okay with her or what

She's just pretending, right?

You were also just pretending, right?

I'm getting kind of worried honestly

so please let me know if you know what's

going on

jfc Brick is dead???

Are you seeing this

You were right I think

Let me know if you are okay

RnBw

hey Replay

I really need your help

I don't think sparkle should have kicked you

out of the group btw

Just pls

if you have any idea what to do

pls tell me

PXL_20221001_153329615.mp4

It's my little sister

I'm scared

15://

"Look," Teresa says to Jason. "You weren't the only one."

She turns her phone to show him a video her friend RnBw sent her. A young girl scrunched in the corner of a leather sofa, gripping her phone, staring straight ahead, not moving.

She clicks to another video that someone posted from an internet café. A man in headphones sits frozen, staring at Brick's offline message on the screen in front of him. The person filming says something in another language, shakes the man by the shoulder, but he doesn't react. The view moves to the next computer over, where another man sits, frozen the exact same way.

Teresa finds other videos, other posts, from all over the country, all over the world. Frantic parents seeking help. Friends, roommates, partners. It's the same report from all of them. Someone they knew was watching Brick's stream and now that person is frozen, alive but unresponsive. Not moving, not speaking, not responding. Just like Jason.

The story has made it to major news outlets, not just the gaming and tech sites. Some megachurch leader in Florida has declared that this is a sign of the coming rapture. Conspiracy theories are running rampant. This is bigger than she'd ever imagined. So many people.

"You really think they're possessed?" Jason asks.

"I do," she says. She shows him the article about Brick's death.

"Shit," he says, frowning down at the phone, face lit from below. He looks up at her, meets her eyes. "What do we do?"

With a mixture of pride and fear, she realizes that she's the big sister again. The one in charge. The one who can fix things. "I don't know, exactly," she says. "You woke up once I disconnected everything."

She pulls up Ozma's stream on her phone. No change. She's still silent and staring. It breaks Teresa's heart to see her that way.

"You could go live," Jason says. "And warn people. Tell them to turn everything off."

"I can't. My account got banned." She clicks away from Ozma, checks KingCoal and Horsegirl. Same thing there.

"Oh." Jason sounds disappointed. "Well, you could just stream somewhere else, couldn't you?"

He's right. There are other platforms she could try. Several of her social media accounts even have rudimentary "Go Live" features.

"I don't know," she says. "It might not be safe. Look at this."

Teresa shows Jason her screen again. She navigates to the "browsing" page, clicks from stream to stream.

At any given moment, there are thousands of streams just on this one platform. Usually, they are all different. People making art, playing music, walking in nature, whispering into the mic, tapping the mic with long fake nails, building bases, shooting zombies, racing cars, crashing cars into other cars, exploring caves, exploring alien planets. People fighting each other, people helping each other, people watching each other. People who are not people but AR anime girls controlled by facial sensors.

But all the streams are the same now. No one is moving. No one is talking. No one is typing or painting or clicking. Games are stalled out at death screens. Avatars run endlessly through their idle animations.

"Is it a trend?" asks Jason. "Are they faking?"

"All of them?"

"I guess not."

"Do you believe me?" Teresa asks him. The same thing she asked Ozma.

"Um. Yeah. I guess, maybe. I don't know." Jason looks uneasy. He's retrieved his phone from the floor, but he hasn't turned it on yet. "Can I text Tyler?"

"Tyler?" Teresa conjures up an image of a small blond boy in a peewee league jersey. He's bigger, now, of course. She saw him out the window just last week, waiting with his bike for Jason to come out and meet him. "Why?"

"I think he might have been watching Brick," Jason says. He's looking at her searchingly. He seems to be waiting for permission. He believes her. She can tell.

"Are you sure you feel okay?" she asks. "Like, your head and everything? No headache?"

"Yeah. I feel fine now. I mean, freaked out a little. But I'm fine."

Is it safe to let him turn his phone on? She isn't sure. The ghost got Brick when he was streaming. He got Hedge and Horse and King when they were streaming. Kyle had followed them when he was alive. Kept following them even after death. He asked them to open a door, and once they did, he found his way in.

But what about Ozma? What about the other streamers?

And what about Jason? What about the thousands of viewers who were watching Brick's stream? They didn't all open doors right before, did they?

Maybe the doors never mattered. Maybe they were just a metaphor. Or maybe the ghost is getting stronger.

"Okay," she tells Jason reluctantly. "Go ahead."

Teresa returns to her phone. She types up instructions.

> Turn off your computers. Turn off your phones.
> Disconnect everything.

She copy-pastes it to all her accounts, all the message boards and forums.

An immediate reply to one of her posts: *you don't seem to have disconnected lol*.

She ignores that. Sends the same instructions in direct messages to everyone she knows in the streaming community, even people she's only talked to once or twice. She replies to Jolley, tries to tell them what she thinks is going on in as clear and succinct a way as possible. She gives RnBw more detailed instructions to wake her sister up.

"Tyler's not responding." Jason looks up from his phone, forehead creased with concern.

"He probably just hasn't seen your texts yet."

It's silly of her to reassure him when she is buzzing with fear herself. She needs to hold herself together. She needs to be strong, somehow, for Jason and for Ozma and for all the others. She doesn't know if she can. Why couldn't this be someone else's responsibility? Someone brave, someone sane.

"I tried calling, too," says Jason. He's up on his feet now, pacing, staring down at his phone. "I think I need to go check on him. He's my best friend."

Teresa feels a stab of jealousy and is immediately ashamed of herself. She wishes Becks were here. She always wishes that, but it hits her extra hard for a moment, a punch to the gut.

"Maybe you should wait until Mom and Dad get home," she says to Jason. "They can give you a ride."

He stops pacing for a moment and scowls at her. "That makes no sense. If he's possessed or something, I've got to save him."

"But it's not—" She stops herself from finishing the sentence. It's *not* safe. Not safe to bike in the dark. Not safe to go outside. But danger found them here. Crawled right through their screens. Nothing is safe. Nowhere is safe. Maybe they need to run away and live off the grid. Go to the National Radio Quiet Zone, swear off the internet forever.

Teresa tries to focus. Jason is watching her. His friend Tyler lives less than a mile away. The two of them are constantly biking to and from each other's houses. "Okay," she says. "Yeah. You know what to do if he's . . . you know what to do, right?"

Jason nods. He starts for the door.

If Ozma lived half a mile away, Teresa would go there too, wouldn't she?

"You could come with me," Jason says, turning.

Teresa hesitates.

"No, never mind." Jason waves a dismissive hand. "Sorry. I know you can't. I mean, you left your room, so I guess I just thought maybe . . ."

She cuts him off. "It's not that."

Well, it is that, but it's not *just* that. Brick died. The possession killed him. It took hours and hours, but if the ghost is getting stronger, maybe it won't take so long with the others.

With Ozma.

"I think I need to go to West Virginia," she says.

KingCoal is live now with 5.1K viewers
Category: Block Game
XSMP—CHILL BASE BUILDING STREAM

KingCoal stares straight ahead, unmoving. His eyes reflect the glowing rectangles of the screen in front of him.

In the game, his avatar stares down at the ground. The view jolts right with a *thwack* sound. Something is attacking him.

> ### Chat
>
> [3:05:00]—move man

Thwack. The screen shifts right. *Thwack.* His hearts are going down, one by one. A screen appears, announcing: "You Died!"

> [3:09:09]—F

There are options to respawn or return to title. His expression doesn't change, but his finger twitches on the mouse. He clicks RESPAWN.

> [3:10:45]—is he going to die irl?
> [3:10:50]—don't say that!

The sequence repeats. An unseen monster attacks him in the game. He dies.

He clicks. He dies.

[3:15:27]—someone should check on him

Clicks. Dies.

[3:17:05]—its only been three hours

And then again.

[3:19:05]—F

And again.

And again.

 Horsegirl4 is live now with 4.8K viewers
Category: Survival Game
NEW MAPS LET'S SEE HOW LONG WE CAN HOLD OUT

Horsegirl sits in the same place they've been sitting for hours now. Black sweatshirt, arms at their sides. Rubber horse mask. We can't see their real face, their real eyes. Just the mask.

They are shaking. It was slight at first, a mere tremor, but it has been growing in intensity.

> **Chat**
>
> [3:13:02]—no one is safe anymore
> [3:13:03]—open the door, chat
> [3:13:05]—time to accept it

They shake all over. The chair is shaking along with them now, shifting on the ground, rolling gently back and forth.

A word, barely audible, spoken quietly and muffled by the mask.

"No."

> [3:13:08]—yes

Their arms fly out in front of them. They seem to be reaching for the mouse, the keyboard, but they miss, and instead bang their hands against the edge of the desk, with enough force that their chair rolls back.

[3:13:10]—nt

They are still shaking, more violently now. They reach up for their mask. They are gripping the bottom edge of it, but it isn't clear what they are trying to do. One moment they seem to be trying to pull it up, the next they seem to be pulling it back down.

[3:13:12]—omg face reveal?
[3:13:12]—take it off!

Their hands are shaking so hard they lose their grip on the mask. They reach out for something on the floor instead. They lift it up. A black cord. The power cord? They are tugging on it, trying to pull it from the unseen socket, perhaps.

[3:13:17]—looks like stream about to end
[3:13:18]—peace out, it's been real

Then they aren't pulling anymore, they are lifting the cord. They are wrapping it around their neck, just underneath the bottom edge of the mask.

[3:13:24]—wtf?
[3:13:25]—I feel like I shouldn't be watching this

They are pulling the cord in a circle. They are pulling on the ends, pulling it tight.

> [3:13:27]—going to get banned for sure

Tighter.

> [3:13:28]—F

Latest Posts

Laura Moore @lmgirl95
My roommate still won't wake up I don't know what do
💬 6   🔁 0   ♥ 15

Replay @replay
Turn off your computers. Turn off your phones. DISCONNECT EVERYTHING.
💬 12   🔁 17   ♥ 102

Laura Moore @lmgirl95
Update: the EMTs are here
💬 1   🔁 0   ♥ 4

Sheyona @LashanaSerene
Everyone beware this is more serious than the mainstream media is making it seem. More people are going to die. This might be a targeted attack of some kind. Deep State? We've got to document this.
💬 8   🔁 23   ♥ 421

Laura Moore @lmgirl95
I can't believe I'm saying this. She flatlined in the ambulance. They couldn't bring her back. Fuck.
💬 15   🔁 2   ♥ 36

What's happening

News · Trending
New Virus?

#ACAB
Trending with swatting

Open the Door

Gaming · Trending
Brick

Technology · Trending
Deadstreaming

Who to follow

@moonshoes . . . follows you

@SudoPi . . . follows you

@rigelus_ . . . follows you

Jolley

So is Ozma in danger?

yes

What do we do?

my brother was catatonic
but as soon as I turned everything off
internet power phone
he woke up
thats the only way I know to fix it
i think I need to go there

Are you up for that?
I thought you couldn't . . .
I mean
You know
Your whole thing

i can try
ive got to at least try

How far are you from where she lives
You're both East Coast right?

not really coast
but yes im one state away

its 1 hr 45

Do you have a car you could use?

no
i cant drive

Anyone who could give you a ride?

i don't think so

Wish I wasn't so far away
Bus?

nothing direct
and nothing until tomorrow

How about a Lyft or Uber or something?

i don't know
ive never done that

I use it all the time out here
That's a bit of a long ride, but some drivers will
do it
You can call them for other people, you know
Just give me your address
I'll send one to you

are you sure?

i mean, i can pay you back.

No way

If you're right, then this is the least I can do

16://

Teresa takes a pill. One of the ones to use only in emergencies, during panic attacks, to calm her down. Usually, she's afraid to take them. They can be dangerous. They can be addictive. They can kill you if you take too much. Usually by the time she's anxious enough to take a pill, she's *too* anxious to take a pill. She keeps the bottle in a box inside another box inside a third box with a lock.

But she opens the box and takes one, now, swallows it dry, quick before she can doubt herself. It's the only way she'll be able to go through with this. She thinks about taking two, but she's worried that will knock her out, and she's got to be clearheaded enough to save Ozma when she gets there.

If she's not too late.

She can't consider that. It will be fine. Ozma will be okay. Jason was okay, wasn't he? Brick held out a long time before . . . but that won't happen to Ozma. It can't happen.

Jolley has called a car for her. Jason is downstairs now. He's going to get his bike and meet her out front. She just needs to go downstairs again. And then she needs to leave the house. And then . . .

The pill feels like maybe it got stuck in her throat. Did it? She swallows. Her throat feels scratchy. Probably nothing. But is she choking? Can she breathe?

She's obviously breathing. In and out. She can feel that, hear it.

Is she really getting any air, though?

Doesn't feel like it.

Her throat burns. She swallows, coughs.

She's fully panicking, but she uses the panic to propel herself out into the hallway. She goes to the bathroom, turns on the water, cups her hands under the faucet and gulps down handfuls, fast and desperate, splashing the water into her mouth before it can trickle through her fingers.

A text comes from Jolley. The first driver canceled but another driver accepted the ride. There's a make and model for the car. A license plate number. A name. Steven.

Is Steven a good driver? A safe driver? Has he had his brakes checked recently? Has he ever killed anyone with his car?

I can't do this, Teresa thinks. *I can't.*

But even as she thinks it, her legs are moving.

She goes downstairs. The pill seems to be kicking in already, making her feel like she is floating down the staircase, swimming through the air. She stops at the front door, beside the coat rack, stares down at her feet, the scratchy welcome mat beneath them, so faded and stained now that the cheery message it once bore is illegible: *All* something something *here* something *ends*. Or is that last word meant to be *friends*? She can't remember.

A few days ago, just coming this far felt impossible, but here she is.

She's pretty sure that the ghost gets to people through screens. Opening the front door right now shouldn't make any difference. Still, her brain can't quite let go of the fear. If there's a chance, even a tiny chance, that doors are dangerous, she doesn't want to risk it. She will cling to any scrap of safety, any scrap of control.

She convinced Jason to go out a window. He had clearly been

skeptical about that, but it looks like he followed her instructions. The nearest window is open, gauzy white curtains billowing in the breeze.

Another text from Jolley. The car is five minutes away.

Teresa crawls through the window, flops awkwardly out the other side like a baby horse being born, and tumbles to the flower bed below. She stands up, brushes the dirt from her jeans.

She's done it. She's on the front lawn now. The window is still open behind her, but ahead and above and to every side, there's just air. Open space yawning wider and wider, stretching out forever.

She'd forgotten on some primal level what it felt like to be exposed this way, without walls all around you, protecting you. A snail out of its shell.

There's too much out here. Too much space, too much noise. She can hear outside sounds from her room, of course, but muffled by wall and window. Now there's nothing between her and the humming power lines, the angry voices from a neighbor's television set turned up loud, the unseen birds shrieking in the trees. She smells motor oil and a faint hint of sewage. The wind brushes her face. She didn't even think to grab a coat. She didn't bring anything except her phone, out of necessity, and the bottle of anxiety pills, which she slipped into her pocket just in case.

Something moves in the corner of her vision. She spins around, but it's just Jason, wheeling his bike around the side of the house.

"Hey," he says, smiling. "You're outside."

"Yeah."

She can feel her panic doing battle with the pill she took. Her heart wants to race but it can't, swaddled in an oversized chemical sweater, muffled by the medicine.

She checks her phone.

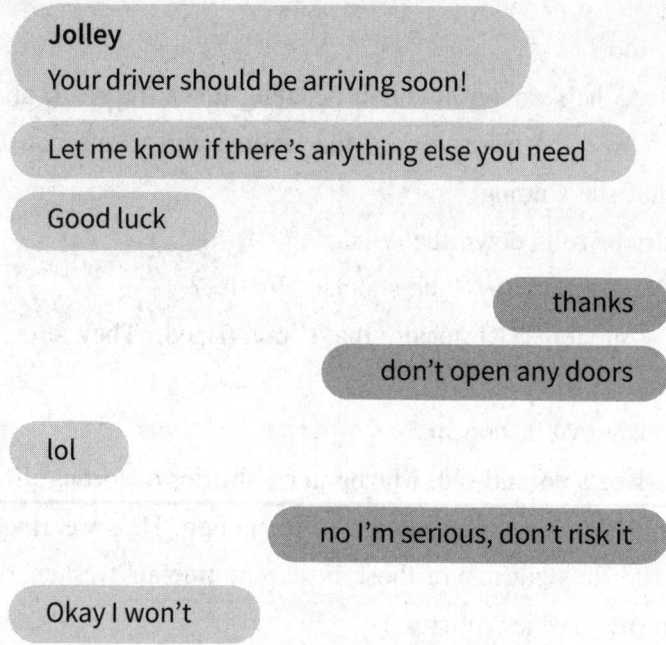

Jolley
Your driver should be arriving soon!

Let me know if there's anything else you need

Good luck

thanks

don't open any doors

lol

no I'm serious, don't risk it

Okay I won't

When she looks back up there's a car slowing to a stop in front of her house.

"Is that your ride?" Jason asks.

She lunges forward and hugs him again. It's an awkward side hug, since he's holding the handlebars of his bike, but he lets her do it. Pats her on the back with one hand, even.

This is happening too fast. She turns to look at the open window. She could go back inside. She could run to her room and close the door. She could wait until her parents come home. She could close her eyes and hide until it's all over.

"You'll need to explain things to Mom and Dad when they get home," she says to Jason.

"I'll try."

"Please be careful."

"You, too."

And then he's off on his bike, pedaling down the road, and she's walking across the lawn, toward the waiting car, trying not to think about what she's doing.

The driver rolls down the window.

"Are you, umm, Joy?" he shouts. "Joe-lee?"

"No, I'm Teresa. I mean, that's my friend. They ordered the ride."

"Oh, okay. Well, hop in."

The driver's not old-old. Maybe in his thirties or forties? She can't really tell. He seems nice enough, safe enough. He's wearing a gray fleece vest. He's got one of those little pine tree air fresheners hanging from the rearview mirror.

She's made it to the curb. She feels like she might come unstuck from the ground at any moment, like gravity will just quit working and she will fly out into the atmosphere.

She reaches one hand toward the backseat door handle, then stops.

"It's unlocked," says the driver.

But it's a door, isn't it? A car door. Does that count? She tries to convince herself that it doesn't matter, that it's safe. She isn't streaming. Isn't even looking at her phone. The ghost can't get her. He seems to have spared her once before, anyway, for reasons she doesn't fully understand. There's no way this door is dangerous.

Still, she can't bring herself to do it.

"Ma'am?" The driver is waiting for her. He sounds confused.

"I'm sorry," she says. "Can you help me?"

She stares down at her hands, as if they are the ones stopping her. The driver gets out of the car and comes around to her side. He opens the car door.

"You okay?" he asks.

"Yes, I'm so sorry. I just . . ." There's no way to explain this. "I don't know. Thank you."

He's got his eyebrows way up, but he waits until she slides into the car. He shuts the door for her. He must think she's an entitled little bitch.

The driver gets back into the driver's seat. There's a large mole on the back of his neck. Has he noticed it? He probably can't see it. Maybe she should mention it? What if it's cancer?

"Going pretty far, huh?" he asks, as he adjusts his phone, which is mounted on the dashboard.

How does she talk to people in real life? She's not prepared for this.

"Um, yeah. Going to my friend's place."

Teresa sends a quick message to Jolley, and then one to her parents, and then she turns the phone off, just to be safe.

"I've never done a ride this long," says the driver, "but it's been a slow night and I figured what the heck." He laughs. "I could really use the money."

"Oh. Well, thanks."

He starts the car.

Teresa's heart rate punches through the barrier of the anxiety pill. She fumbles the bottle from her pocket and takes another one. She hopes the driver doesn't see.

She is in a car. A moving car. It's been months. Months and months. After the accident, her parents would drive her to doctor's appointments, but she had a panic attack every time she got in the car, so as soon as she could, she stopped. She decided she would never ride in a car ever again.

The car is moving. The car is speeding up. They probably aren't going that fast—this is a residential area—but it feels way too fast to Teresa.

The seats are leather. There's a faint scent of pine. She tries to focus on that. Tries to pretend that she's actually in a small, safe room.

"So, what do you do?" the driver asks.

Small talk. How normal people distract themselves from the unbearable horror of being alive. Teresa digs her fingernails into her palms. Should she say she's a student? Will the driver kick her out if he finds out she's under eighteen?

"I'm a livestreamer," she says. "So like I play games and—"

"Oh, heck yeah!" the driver cuts her off. "I know all about livestreaming. I'm not *that* old." He chuckles. "I've seen that guy, Hedgelord. You ever seen him? He does these pranks that are off the wall."

Teresa digs her fingernails in harder. "Oh," she says. Does the driver not know what happened? She doesn't want to be the one to tell him. "Did you see his latest?"

"Nah, I usually just watch the edited-down versions. Sometimes if it's a slow day I'll tune in between rides, but I can't watch when I'm driving now, can I? Eyes on the road!"

He chuckles again. Teresa wishes he wouldn't.

"I've got a daughter," he says.

"Cool," Teresa says uncertainly. Her phone is off, but she can feel it like an itch in her pocket. She wants to turn it on. To check.

"It's tough because I don't want her to get exposed to a lot of the stuff online, but how can I keep her from it entirely? You know, it's just part of modern life now."

"Yeah," Teresa says. "It is."

The second pill is hitting much harder, stacked on top of the first. She mumbles something about wanting to rest, leans her head back against the seat, closes her eyes.

She drifts on the edge of drugged sleep. Becks is sitting beside her laughing, and then she's gone. The driver has the radio on and there's a man talking about a distant war. Someone is breathing on her neck. Someone is touching the back of her neck.

She jolts awake to the sound of a phone buzzing. Her hand goes to her pocket, but her phone is still off.

It's the driver's phone. In the rearview mirror, she can see his eyes glance over at it. *Eyes on the road*, she thinks. *Eyes on the road*.

They pass a paved lot full of sheds and shacks and mobile homes for sale. So many doors. They pass a deer crossing sign. A line of orange-and-white-striped cones. Everything warning danger.

They pull to a stop at a red light. Steven reaches over and checks his phone.

"Weird," he says.

"What?" she says though she doesn't really want to know.

"Oh, didn't realize you were awake back there. You said your name is Teresa, right?"

"Yes."

"There's a message for you."

Unknown number
tell Replay to turn on her phone

I mean Teresa

tell her I want to talk

tell her I need a favor

tell her I'm burning through the others too fast

tell her to go live

who is this?

she knows who this is

and I know who you are

Steven

look I don't know what this is about

or how you even got this number

but I don't stand for any bullshit

so back off buddy

you'll regret that

17://

"Turn off your phone." Teresa's voice is shaking. She knows she probably sounds hysterical, but she can't help it.

"I blocked his number."

"Just turn off your phone. I don't want him to find me."

"Who is this guy?" The driver looks at her in the rearview. "Ex-boyfriend?"

"No. Just a . . . stalker, I guess. Please turn it off."

"I need it for the GPS, darling. We're nearly there, just hold on." He turns up the radio. The message is clear. Leave me alone, let me drive. Maybe he is regretting picking up this ride. Teresa hopes Jolley tipped well.

She should pay them back. She will, if she makes it through this. Although she's pretty sure Jolley *is* kind of rich. They've never exactly talked about money, but there's little things that make it clear. The way Jolley's room looks onstream. Their top-tier gaming setup.

The driver's phone buzzes again. A call this time. Unknown number. It rattles the phone holder. The driver glances at it, then dismisses it with a swipe.

Teresa is picking at the skin of her palms, worrying the lines there, tracing them over and over again, digging in with her fingernails, scratching until the flesh is red and raw. What does she do? What *can* she do?

The ghost can reach her here. He can reach her anywhere.

A few minutes later, the phone rings again.

"Darn spam calls," the driver mutters, dismissing it again.

Despite everything, Teresa wants to turn her phone back on. She wants to find out what's happened in the last hour and a half. Maybe Ozma is all right. Maybe she woke up on her own. Maybe it was all a big misunderstanding. Maybe there's a reasonable explanation.

The car pulls to a stop. Not a red light this time, but a train crossing, with the warning arm down and bells ringing.

The driver's phone buzzes again. He grabs it from the dashboard holder.

"Don't!" Teresa shouts.

"Excuse me?" Steven turns to look at her. He looks tired and a little angry. He looks like maybe he'll just drop her on the side of the road if she doesn't stop making strange demands.

"I . . ." What can she say? Should she tell him there's a ghost, tell him he's putting her in danger? It sounds unbelievable.

Before she can decide, the driver swipes the phone, presses it to his ear. "Hello."

Teresa digs her fingernails harder into her palms. Maybe it really is a spam call. Maybe it's fine and she is worrying too much. She's good at that. She does it all the time.

"What?" says the driver. "Why would I do that?"

Maybe it's someone he knows.

"Who the hell are you, anyway?" He glances out the window. "No, I don't believe you. You're just messing with me. I don't see anything out there."

He reaches for the car door handle.

"Stop!" Teresa tries to lunge forward, to grab the phone from his hand, but her seat belt holds her back. "Steven!"

He opens the door.

Teresa fights to get her seat belt unhooked.

The driver drops the phone. He slumps forward. His head hits the wheel. The car horn blares.

This isn't happening. It can't be happening.

Teresa reaches forward, shakes his shoulder. "Steven? Wake up! Please!"

And she's back for a moment, to that night a year ago. She's alone in a wrecked car on a dark road, Becks unconscious beside her.

Teresa feels a scream building up inside her, but she pushes it down, pushes the memories down.

What now? Should she get out and run? She doesn't know where they are. It's just a forested road. No buildings nearby. Nothing.

The horn is so loud it makes it hard to think clearly. What does she do, what does she do?

She climbs into the front passenger seat, over the center console, pushes the driver upright. The horn cuts out, thank god, though the railroad crossing bells continue to ring. The car doesn't move, the driver's foot still pressing down on the brake.

She tries to prop him back against the seat. He's so heavy, a dead weight. There's a red line where his forehead hit the steering wheel. His eyes are open and staring, just like Jason and Brick. And reflected in each pupil, a glowing rectangle. A light that should not be there.

That night in the car a year ago, Becks woke up.

She opened her eyes. She blinked at Teresa, confused. *Your nose is bleeding*, Becks said. *Your head is bleeding*, Teresa said back. And then she started laughing. Just absolutely lost it. She couldn't stop. Becks looked confused for a moment but then she laughed too. They were alive. They had survived. It would be fine.

Teresa leans over and searches for the driver's phone now, scrabbling around the passenger seat footwell, the console. She spots it, finally, a glint of glass down by his feet. It's an awkward angle, but she stretches, reaches blindly.

Her fingers close around the phone. There's a jolt. The car starts moving.

She straightens up, flooded with a new panic. She must have nudged the driver's foot off the brake pedal. They are trundling forward slowly, the red-and-white-striped barrier growing closer and brighter in the headlights.

Oh god. This is how she dies. Smashing through a crossing, crushed by an oncoming train. She doesn't hear one or see one, but it must be nearby, right? Death is coming down the tracks, death is coming too fast to stop.

Shit shit shit shit *shit*.

She's too much in her head, drowning in her thoughts. There's no time for that. She's got to act.

She grabs the wheel, tries to swerve. Steven falls sideways heavily, slumping against her, knocking her hands away from the wheel. She pushes him away. The car is headed for a different part of the train tracks now, bypassing the warning arm entirely. She hasn't driven in a year. She doesn't know what to do.

The parking brake! Her hands are shaking so hard she can barely grab it, barely press the button at the top. She yanks the lever back.

The car stops.

She can hear herself gasping for air in the quiet of the car.

A train whistle screams. And then the train comes, a thunderous rush, rattling reality into little pieces, drowning out all thought. The car shakes with the force of the train's passage, but Teresa managed to stop it a few feet from the tracks. Safe.

She feels the driver's phone buzz against her thigh. She'd almost forgotten it, but she picks it up, glances down. Messages are flooding in fast.

I see you

I know you

I get you

You get me

Let's collab

We can get so many views

Everyone in the world will watch

You watched

You saw me die

You will help me

Help me

You have to

You don't have a choice

The train cars flash by, too fast to focus on, a blur of colors.

The driver twitches.

"Steven?"

He jerks, flails an arm. His movements are spasmodic, seemingly without direction. She needs to turn the phone off, break the connection. She feels for the power button.

Something smacks her in the face. A bright flash of pain.

The driver. His arm. He hit her. She is stunned, holding on to her throbbing nose.

He grabs the phone before she can react. With a quick snap of the wrist, he throws it out the driver's side door, which is still open a crack. Teresa watches the phone land softly in the grass a few feet away, beside the train tracks. She should go and get it, turn it off.

But she can't open her door, can she? She had begun to think she was being overcautious about doors, that it had become another needless compulsion. But clearly the ghost asked the driver to open the door. And when he complied, that let the ghost in. Maybe it's not the door itself, but doing what the ghost asks you to do? She doesn't know. But she's trapped in here, unless she wants to try to crawl past him.

The driver turns to look at her. His expression is entirely flat and neutral. Empty. He opens his mouth. It seems like he's trying to talk, but all that comes out is a strained groan.

Teresa feels beyond afraid. She feels blank with fear. Like she's been erased. She isn't a person anymore, just a raw nerve.

The driver is reaching for her. But his hands are shaking. His arm falls limp back to his side. He tries to speak again, and this time, he just barely manages to rasp out something resembling words. "He's . . . fighting."

"Let him go," says Teresa. She whispers it, her voice made small by fear. She presses herself against the car door behind her.

The driver doesn't answer. He doesn't blink. Doesn't move. Whatever struggle is going on inside his head, it isn't visible out here.

The car handle is digging into her back. Should she just open it? Open the door and run? The ghost hasn't asked her to do it, so maybe it is safe.

"Why are you doing this?" she asks the driver. "What do you want?"

"Eyes," he rasps.

His body spasms. He folds over on himself. He makes a retching sound. Teresa is worried he is choking, but she can't move, can only watch.

When he straightens up, though, his expression is as flat and neutral as ever. When he speaks, his tone is equally flat.

"Turn on your phone," he says. His voice is clearer now.

"No!" She tries to back up even further, but there's no room. She can't turn on her phone. She can't open the door.

"Do it." He sounds entirely emotionless, which somehow scares her more than if he sounded angry.

She stares at him. She can't, right? She can't do anything he says. There's still a way out of this. If she can just dive past him, quick, and then out the open driver-side door. She can find his phone, turn it off, break the connection.

He smiles at her. A horrible smile, like the corners of his mouth are being yanked upward by strings. The rectangles of impossible light glint in his eyes.

His arm shoots forward.

She ducks, but he wasn't reaching for her. His fist collides with the rearview mirror.

The mirror tilts, the pine tree air freshener swings wildly, but the glass doesn't break. The driver punches it again. Teresa cowers, covering her head, immobile with fear. He hits the mirror again and again and finally it shatters. Bright shards scatter across the dashboard. Some land on Teresa's jeans. She's pressing herself as far back against the car door as she can.

The driver picks up the largest shard of mirror from where it fell into the cupholder. His knuckles are bleeding. He holds up the shard between them. Teresa can see her reflection in it for a moment. Her wide and terrified eyes.

And then he plunges it into his eye. Into the driver's eye. Steven's eye.

Teresa watches him do it. She wishes she'd blinked or looked away, but she watches. She sees the jagged edge pierce the soft surface. It happens so fast. Easy as a soft-boiled egg.

The sound of it. She'll never get it out of her mind. A wet *pop*. A *squish*.

He yanks the shard back out. Blood comes out in a trickle at first, pooling on his lower lashes, and then gathering force, waterfalling over the lid and down the cheek.

"Do it," he says, eerily calm. The blood runs over his lips, into his mouth. It stains his teeth red.

"Stop," she says. "Please." She is crying, the tears running down her own cheeks.

He is looking at her with his good eye, and there is an expression there that isn't blank anymore. He looks scared and sad. Is that Steven looking out? Or is it Kyle?

"Your phone," he says wetly.

"Please," she says again. "Stop. Stop."

He does the other eye.

She lunges forward, trying to stop him, to grab his arm, but it is too late.

The shard of mirror, already slick with blood, slices through the sclera, the pupil. Both his eyes are a ragged mess. Pink and red. Smashed grapes. It's all her fault.

"I'll do it." She is sobbing now. "I'll do it."

He pushes the shard farther, deep into the socket. Then he slumps forward, arms limp, hands face up on his lap. The blood pours into his open palms.

LIVE 👁 47

Replay is running down a dark street. She is
breathing hard. It looks like she's been crying.

> "Hello? Is this working?
> Can you hear me?"

She holds the phone in front of her. Our view
is shaky, bobbing up and down. Sometimes we
see her face from below, sometimes we can't
see anything at all.

> "I have a message. For anyone
> who is watching."

She passes under a streetlight. Pauses. Looks
behind her. Is there someone there? It's too
dark to see. The video quality is poor. Pixelated,
full of noise.

> "Um. I don't know why he—
> I don't know, but I have to—"

She runs again, stumbling over her words and
then her feet. She sinks to her knees, bringing
us down with her.

She looks at her phone, at us. Her face is half-shadowed. Tears pool on her lower lashes, then fall. We see this only because they catch the light, sparkling.

She seems to be reading something, a text maybe. Something we can't see.

"This is a message from a—from someone else. He wants me to tell you this."

She struggles to her feet, keeps walking.

"He says none of you would watch him before."

Tears still shine on her cheeks, but her voice is steadier.

"He says all of you will watch now. Whether you want to or not."

Her eyes dart between the phone and her surroundings.

"He says stop focusing on Brick, Brick doesn't matter, he was just a means to an end. Um. He says he has everyone's eyes. I don't know what that means. I—"

She turns around quickly, looks behind her, as if she's heard something or seen something.

The camera's phone struggles to focus on the darkness behind her.

She turns back. She walks faster, but she speaks slowly, pausing between each line.

"He wants you all to know his name."

We can hear her breathing, fast and ragged.

"Kyle Schaeffer. He wants you to remember him. He wants you to know him."

The hand holding the phone seems to be shaking. The image shakes along with it.

"He wants you to watch him."

She stops walking, squats down. She's looking at something in front of her, but the phone camera remains focused on her face. She's feeling around on the ground.

"He—um, he wants me to say this, but I have to—I'm sorry."

She straightens up. We see she is holding a
large rock. She rears back and throws it.

The sound of glass shattering.

        "He says to open the door."

She walks forward. We hear glass crunching
under her feet.

        "He says to let him in."

18://

Teresa climbs through the window she broke. The shattered glass still clinging to the frame snags her jeans, tears them.

She is lucky. The glass only barely grazes her thigh. It stings, but she's not bleeding much.

She is lucky, they weren't that far from Ozma's house when the driver . . . when he . . .

She is lucky. She survived. Back in the woods, she was the one who survived. And now, for the second time, she got out of the car and walked away. She is still alive.

She is still live.

"I'm only doing what I have to do," she says to the viewers on her phone. "Please forgive me."

A message pops up at the top of the screen.

Say it again.

She is in Ozma's cousin's house now. At least she hopes she is, hopes this is the right house, and no one is calling the police right now. Maybe she should have just knocked, but she doesn't feel like she has time. Everything has gone wrong. Everything is hurtling out of control.

Back by the train tracks, she had turned on her phone. She had called 911, but the call cut out abruptly after a few seconds. *Go live*, the ghost told her, so she did, on one of her social media accounts to get around the ban.

"Open the door," she says. "Everyone watching this now. Open the door."

She can atone for this later. Her only hope now, she thinks, is to follow along and hope the ghost won't realize what else she's trying to do.

She can't give up, can't leave Ozma alone.

In the woods, a year ago, she and Becks had climbed out of the crumpled car. Teresa was afraid, but not of the right things. She was afraid of getting in trouble. Afraid that her parents would be angry. She was so naïve then.

The trees rustled in the wind. Becks leaned over and vomited in the dirt. Teresa tried to find her phone. It had gone flying off the dashboard when they crashed. It must have hit the windshield too, because when she found it in the backseat, the screen was smashed and broken.

Where's your phone? she asked Becks.

I don't know.

Well, find it! Shit.

Teresa was restless, buzzing. Electric with adrenaline. She paced around the car. She needed to move, to go somewhere, to do something.

I'll go back to the main road, she said, already walking away, *I'll flag down another car.*

Wait, said Becks. *Don't just leave me here.* She was sitting on the ground beside the car, huddled, knees drawn close.

You can come with me.

Just stay here. Stay with me. Please.

I'll be right back.

And Teresa left. She left Becks there, alone.

She thought the bad part was over. She thought they were safe. She didn't know that danger can be invisible, quiet and soft as a cat padding through the night. We are all mice all the time. We are never safe.

The basement in Ozma's cousin's house is lit by a bare bulb. Someone removed the door from its hinges in the past. Teresa descends the rickety staircase.

"He says not to fight it," she tells her viewers. "He says to open the door and let him in."

Her eyes dart to the hulking shapes of furnace and washer, the stacks of cardboard boxes, the old door leaning against a wall, and then back to her phone. Someone is standing behind her.

She whips around and sees nothing but a workbench covered in paint cans, but on her phone the shadow figure is there. It is Kyle. Or whatever is left of him. She thinks she can almost make out his gray shirt.

A ghost.

He's a ghost.

Part of Teresa wants to turn, to confront him, but her best chance, she thinks, is to stay live, to keep cooperating, to keep saying the things he wants her to say. She needs to save Ozma. She needs to redeem herself.

She walked away once and she will never forgive herself.

Stay with me. Please.

"I'm sorry," she says to her phone. "I'm just doing what I have to do."

The figure is moving toward her. She finds the breaker box, pries it open. It's not too different from the one in her own house. Lots of little switches. *Fridge. LV room. Up bed.* One big switch.

On the phone, she can see a shadowy arm reaching for her. A shadowy hand, inches from her own arm.

She switches the power off and at the same time presses the button on her phone.

The overhead lights go off, plunging the basement into darkness. The phone takes a moment longer. Just before the screen shuts off entirely, she feels something brushing her face. She hears a voice, whispering in her ear.

Kyle's voice. The same voice she'd heard in the video of his death. So close.

The words are clear. She doesn't want to hear them, but she does.

She throws her phone into the dark. It hits something with a *clang*.

It is pitch-dark in the basement now. Dead silent. She thinks she hears something rustling faintly. Scuttling. Cockroaches? Spiders? She runs for where she thinks the stairs are, stumbles in the dark, catches herself. She keeps thinking she feels something brushing against her neck, but when she tries to brush it away, there's nothing there.

She makes it up the basement stairs, but the first floor isn't much brighter. This house is down a dead-end street, at the very deadest end of it. She finds her way to the other staircase, climbs to the second story.

"Ozma?" she calls. There are three doors up here. Two closed, one open. She goes through the open one, but it's only a bathroom.

No doors. She can't let go of that. She needs to be in control of something. Needs at least one rule to keep her safe. Or to give her the illusion of control, at least, the illusion of safety.

The bathroom window faces the front of the house, where there's a porch. She opens it, climbs out, shuffles carefully along the slanted porch roof, hugging the wall. She should be afraid of falling, but she's passed through fear, come out the other side. She reaches the next window and peers through. Feels a rush of agonizing relief.

Ozma is sitting at her desk. She's staring at the blank screen of her computer.

Teresa pauses for a moment, hand on the glass. She can't believe she's truly here. Can't believe that's actually Ozma on the other side of the glass. The princess in the mirror. Ozma's white-blond hair almost glows in the darkness. Teresa had always hoped she and Ozma could meet in person someday, though she never thought it would be like this.

She pushes the window open and climbs through, then closes it behind her.

Ozma doesn't turn or react. She's still not moving. She's breathing, though. Teresa checks that first, tries not to look at the glowing rectangles in her friend's eyes. She searches the room for Ozma's phone. It must be here, keeping the connection going. She knocks several things off the desk in her haste, trips over a cord on the floor, growing frantic.

She finds it finally, in the pocket of Ozma's sweatshirt. She has to get up close to her, to touch her.

"Sorry," she says. "If you can hear me."

She pulls the phone out and she doesn't even let herself glance at the screen. She just presses the power button hard, hands shaking.

Ozma jolts in the chair.

Teresa backs up, uncertain, thinking of the driver. Steven.

"Who's there?" Ozma asks, spinning around. She looks confused, frightened. The strange light in her eyes is gone.

Teresa is so glad to hear her voice that for a moment she can barely speak. "Just me," she says softly.

"Replay?"

It's really Ozma. Her face, her voice. But not on the phone, not on the computer.

"You're real," says Teresa. It's a silly thing to say, but it's all she can think of.

"Are you?" Ozma stands up from her chair and stumbles. Teresa moves forward to catch her, but Ozma steadies herself.

"Are you okay?" Teresa asks.

"I don't know. What are you doing here? How did you get here?"

"I took a Lyft."

"But you can't leave the house!"

"I know," Teresa says, and then she is crying. "But the ghost had you and I had to come save you because you weren't moving and I didn't know what else to do and Brick is dead." The words pour out of her, as uncontrollable as the tears. "The ghost killed him and I was so scared he would kill you too. He's everywhere. We have to get away, I think, because he can move through screens. We have to go where there's no internet or phones or anything, like the middle of the desert or an island. That place with the telescopes, maybe. The quiet zone. We have to—"

She runs out of breath, gasps for air. She tries to speak more but subsides into sobs instead. Big, loud, ugly open-mouthed sobs.

Ozma crosses the distance between them. She wraps her arms around Teresa's shoulders and squeezes.

Teresa freezes for a moment. She's not used to touching people anymore.

And then she relaxes into the hug, wraps her arms around Ozma's waist. She presses her face into Ozma's sweatshirt, mumbles an incoherent apology for getting it wet. Her whole body shakes with sobs. Ozma just holds her tight, and Teresa holds her back. She's real. They're both real, here together.

She cries until she can't cry anymore, until she is wrung out. Still, she doesn't let go.

"I can't believe you came all the way here," Ozma says into her hair.

"I had to." Teresa's voice is raw and whispery from all the crying.

Ozma moves away, then, and Teresa feels the loss acutely. She resists the urge to fling herself forward and cling.

"Just a second," says Ozma. She rummages around in a desk drawer, produces a vanilla-scented candle and a book of matches. She lights the candle, which casts a gentle flickering light around the room. Ozma sits on the floor, candle in front of her, and gestures for Teresa to join.

Teresa sits. She reaches out, a little nervous, but Ozma takes her hand without hesitation.

"You were right," Ozma says. "The whole time."

Her glitter eyeshadow sparkles in the light of the candle. She looks tired but in an unbearably glamorous way. Teresa can't stop looking at her, drinking in the sight of her. She's seen Ozma's face many, many times before, of course, but always on a screen, always at a distance. The screen flattens things. Ozma looks different in real life. More complicated, more wonderful.

"I wish I hadn't been," says Teresa.

"Brick is dead?"

"Yes."

Ozma stares into the flame of the candle. "I . . . I thought I was dead. I thought I'd died. I couldn't move and everything was dark. There was this voice whispering to me. Telling me let go, to give in. But I didn't want to." She turns to look at Teresa. "And then you were here."

She squeezes Teresa's hand and Teresa squeezes back. Now that they've reached each other, she never wants to let go. She is in awe of the delicate bones of Ozma's hand, her long, thin fingers. She rubs a thumb over Ozma's knuckles. Ozma glances down.

"Sorry," Teresa says, suddenly self-conscious. She starts to pull her hand away, but before she can, Ozma leans forward and kisses her.

Ozma is the fifth person Teresa has kissed. Preceding her are two guys Teresa didn't really like that much, a girl from camp two summers ago, and Becks once when they were younger, just to see what it was like. But this feels different from any of them. The other kisses didn't feel that dissimilar, really, than putting a hand to her lips. Just a simple sensation. Nice, but nothing special.

This is different. Sure, the angle is a little awkward and their noses bump together, but when their mouths meet, Teresa feels a spark shoot from her lips right down the center of her body. She closes her eyes. She leans in. She wants this kiss to keep going forever.

Ozma pulls away first. "Was that okay?"

"Yes," says Teresa. She feels a little drunk. She remembers something suddenly. "I broke your window. Downstairs. The ghost has this thing about opening doors so that seemed like the only safe way to get inside. I'm sorry."

Ozma laughs. "That doesn't matter. You saved my life."

Teresa feels a stab of horror. What if she hadn't made it here? What if she hadn't been able to save her? She thinks of what the ghost said, right before she shut off her phone. Thinks of the words he whispered in her ear. Thinks of Becks.

She doesn't want to think about that right now. She doesn't want to think about anything. She's very, very tired, but she doesn't want to sleep. She wants to stay in this moment forever, sitting in the warm glow of the candle, holding Ozma's hand.

Despite herself, she yawns. "Sorry," she says again.

"It's late," says Ozma. "You should stay here tonight. I can make up the couch if you'd like."

"Okay," says Teresa, but neither of them is willing to let go of the other's hand, so after Ozma blows out the candle, they crawl into Ozma's bed together. In the darkness, they pull each other close.

It feels right. It feels real. Teresa feels safe, for the first time in a long time. She is fully here, in this moment. A hand brushing her knee. Warm skin. Fluttering breath. A faint scent of strawberry shampoo. The pressure of Ozma's arm around her, keeping her steady.

They touch each other, hesitantly at first, and then urgently. They kiss again, longer and slower. It feels so good not to think, to just give over to presence and pleasure.

Teresa didn't know she could feel this way. In her body for once, not outside it. Lit up from the inside. That spark from their earlier kiss building up into a fire. Keeping her warm. Keeping her here.

The two of them fall asleep wrapped around each other.

Hours later, Teresa jolts awake, heart hammering.

Ozma is still there, asleep, rolled over and facing away. Teresa can feel her breathing, the reassuring rise and fall, the slight heat where their backs touch. She'd like to return to the feeling from a few hours ago, she'd like to reach for Ozma, to touch her, to melt into sensation.

But she can't. She is not here, not in the present. She is far away. She is back in the car, staring into the pulpy mess of the driver's ruined eyes. She is climbing over him. She is wiping the blood from her hands onto the grass.

It had seemed bad enough in the moment, but the shock or the anxiety pill must have been taking the edge off, delaying the real impact so she could keep going.

Now it is here. The fear is here. A wave of horror crashing down on her.

She tries to go back to sleep, but it's no use.

The moment she closes her eyes she is back in the car. She is watching, frozen, as the driver stabs the glass into his eyes, over and over.

And then she's in a different car, a different memory. She sees the flash of the white deer. She sees the wall of trees. She is trying to turn, trying to change this, to stop it from happening.

She is alone. She is walking back up the dark road, much later, after failing to find help. She reaches the car and she sees her again. Becks. Eyes closed, head leaned back against the bumper. There is only a little blood on her forehead, already dried black, tangled in her hair. She looks all right. She looks like she is only sleeping.

But inside her skull, things are swollen and torn. Her brain is bleeding. She'd hit her head hard against the side of the car when they crashed.

Teresa didn't know that. She hadn't known. She tried to shake her awake. The worst possible thing to do. She shook her and when she didn't wake up, she shook her harder. She screamed and screamed until her voice was gone.

Help came, eventually. A car. A siren. A stretcher. The whoosh of the hospital's automatic door, the blinding white light. Becks never woke up. Teresa never got to say goodbye, never got to say she was sorry.

She was the one who convinced Becks to come out that night. She was the one driving, the one who crashed the car. There was no way around it.

She killed her best friend.

She killed her.

Teresa climbs out of bed. Quiet, trying not to wake Ozma. She opens the bedroom door without even pausing. There is a stronger need, a stronger compulsion.

She is thinking of the voice she heard in the basement, just before she cut the power. She is thinking of what Kyle said.

There are more ghosts here, he had whispered in her ear. *I'm not alone.*

Becks
Last Year

up for a drive tonight?

I don't know

I've got so much homework

becks come on

please

I'm barely halfway through the reading

and I haven't even started the calc stuff

if im stuck in my room another minute

im gonna lose it

seriously

today really sucked

i need this

sorry your day sucked:(

pleeeeeeeeeeaaaase

ugh, okay fine

a short one tho

heck yeah!!!

pick you up in like 15

ur the coolest

😎

Becks

Today

are you in there somewhere?

i know this is insane

i know im probably talking to myself

i never even believed in ghosts

you were the one who believed in that stuff

but

some things have happened lately

wild things

i don't know what to believe anymore

i'm not sure it's even safe to be doing this

but ive got to try

are you out there?

if you are i just need to tell you

im so sorry about everything

i wish you were still here

i wish i could go back

I wish I could change what happened

i would give anything

hey

oh

oh my god

becks?

is that really you?

it's me

i'm imagining this

i must be

are you still there?

yes

becks

you're dead

i know

you do?

yeah

but we can still talk

oh becks

where are you

in the dark

how do i reach you

turn on your camera

so i can see you

oh my god

okay

did that work?

Yeah

I see you

turn on the video, then i can hear you too

okay i did it

you can talk out loud now

yes

I've missed you too

Don't cry

It's okay now

No I forgive you

I mean it

It's okay

You can see me too, if you want

there's a way

are you sure?

Okay

If you're sure

you have to trust me

you have to do what I say

do you trust me?

19://

She is in the living room, hunched over on the couch. She is holding her phone in her hands. She went and got it from the basement. Turned it on. She had to try. If there was even the smallest chance, the tiniest sliver of hope.

The whole world is just the screen, now. The words she is reading. The miraculous words.

She whispers to her phone. "I trust you."

> Look behind you

She looks.

There is nothing there. The wall. A framed photo of a flower.

She turns back to the phone. It's recording video, set to selfie mode so that she sees herself. And there, on the screen, in the camera's view, is a door. Behind her. Behind the sofa. Set into the wall where no door should be, just as it was back in her room.

> do you see it?

"Yes."

Open it

"Becks, I-I can't. It's dangerous. There's this other ghost. Kyle. He's hurting people."

i know

I've seen all of it

i've been watching you

but you can do it

I know you can

you've faced so many of your fears

you can face this one too

I'm so proud of you

Teresa was already crying. Tears of joy and disbelief, but now she's a mess. Her nose is running. She's holding back sobs. She's cried too much already today. The skin of her face feels raw.

come through the door

I can tell you in person then

we can see each other again

Teresa sets the phone down, slides the couch out of the way. She does it quietly, so that she won't wake Ozma.

She needs this. Even if it is only for a few minutes. A few seconds. One more memory. One more chance.

She pushes the sofa to the side. A gray stain, previously hidden, mars the beige carpet. Teresa picks up her phone again.

She has to keep her eyes on the screen instead of the wall. On the wall there is nothing. On the screen there is a white door with a silver knob. She reaches out, watching her own hand on the phone's small screen. She closes her hand around the doorknob. She can feel it, though she can't see it in real life. On the screen, she watches herself turn the handle and open the door.

The wall in front of her is still blank. On the screen, though, there is a hallway. The beige carpet of the living room gives way to a wooden floor. The walls are gray. It's dark in the hallway. Too dark to see what's at the end of it.

A slight draft blows out from the open door. Teresa can feel it prickle her skin. Her eyes dart back and forth from the wall to the screen. It's too weird. From one view there's nothing there. If she steps forward, she thinks she'll just smack into the wall.

She closes her eyes. She steps forward.

She doesn't hit the wall, but there is a sort of resistance, as though the air is a liquid. Her limbs feel heavy. Pressure builds in her head. She can't pass through.

Let go. She doesn't hear the words so much as feel them in her mind. *Let go.*

So she does. It is so easy to let go of herself. She does it all the time. She does it automatically. It's like breathing.

She takes another step, and there is no resistance this time. She walks forward into the dark, hears her footsteps echo.

She opens her eyes. She is no longer in the living room of Ozma's cousin's house. She is not in the dark hallway, either. She's in a different room. Small, dim, lit only by a computer sitting on a desk across from her, the screen a blank glowing white.

She's seen this place before. The angle was different, but she recognizes the contours of the dresser to her left, a trophy sitting on top. She recognizes the computer chair. She recognizes the sickly quality of the light.

Kyle's room.

She spins around. Behind her there is a doorway and beyond it a dark hallway, just like in the video.

No. She won't believe it. This can't be his room. Why would Becks lead her here? Was she lying? Was she—

No. Teresa refuses to accept it. It isn't possible. It isn't fair. Becks was back. Teresa wanted so badly to believe that she was back.

She lunges forward, intending to run back down the hallway, hoping that will return her to Ozma's place, but the toe of her sneaker hits something soft and she chokes back a scream.

A body lies on the floor at her feet.

Kyle's body.

Limbs splayed stiff and awkward, face rigid and waxy. This is the same spot where she'd seen him fall in the recording.

She backs up, overcome with horror. It is awful here. A layer of white dust coats almost every surface, little snowdrifts of lint and dead skin. The air is thick with the smell of body odor, unwashed laundry. Something worse beneath that, too, which she realizes only now is the smell of rot. Of death.

Teresa covers her mouth, tries not to breathe too much. She thinks she will be sick.

Kyle's body moves.

His fingers scrabble at the matted gray carpet. He pulls himself up to sitting. Color rushes back to his face. His eyes meet hers. He smirks.

"Got you," Kyle says. His voice sounds like it did on the video. Like it did in the basement, whispering in her ear.

He climbs to his feet, his movement jerky and unnatural. His joints make crackling sounds, like empty protein bar wrappers.

Teresa scrambles backward, though there's nowhere to go. The whole right side of the room is oddly empty. Just darkness and dust. There's no bed. The only furniture in the room is the desk with the computer and the dresser with the dusty trophy.

"Where's Becks?" Teresa asks, panic rising. She knows the answer already. Knew it the moment she recognized this room, but she doesn't want to let go. That little sliver of light in the dark. That cataclysmic joy she'd felt when she saw three dots on the screen, saw that Becks was typing. Like a door, opening.

And now it has slammed closed.

Kyle—his body, his ghost—sneers at her. "Don't be an idiot."

Teresa runs. She darts past Kyle, through the doorway, into the hallway beyond. Into the darkness. She is running as fast as she can. She hasn't run like this in months, pumping her legs, arms swinging, desperate and fast and free.

This hallway is longer than it should be. It just keeps going, the blank walls stretching on and on. She is slowing down, though she doesn't want to.

She is walking.

Each step seems harder than the last. The air is too heavy.

Just push through, she thinks, but even her thoughts feel heavy.

Where is she going? She's looking for someone, maybe.

Becks. Is Becks here? She's trying to reach Becks. Or, no.

Ozma. She's trying to reach Ozma.

Or is it someone else? Who is she looking for?

Who is she?

The hallway looks endless ahead of her. She takes another step, struggling, her muscles shaking with effort.

She can't keep going.

She gives up.

It is so easy to give up. To let go. She turns around.

One step and she's back in Kyle's room. The dark hallway is behind her now. Ahead of her, the dust and the desk and Kyle, who is sitting at his computer. The screen in front of him is still all white, bright and empty as a field of snow.

"You can't run," he says without turning. "There's nowhere to go."

He types something, clicks a few times. The view shifts on-screen.

It takes Teresa a moment to understand. The blank whiteness on the screen before was a wall. She can see, now, where that wall ends, where it intersects with a beige carpeted floor. She can see a stain on the carpet. She can see the toes of a pair of sneakers, as if she was looking down at them.

Her sneakers.

"No," she says.

"You opened the door," says Kyle. He sounds smug, triumphant. He spins his chair around to face her. "You let me all the way in."

Teresa takes a step back. Her thoughts are just a hiss of panic. What has she done? How could she be so foolish?

Kyle's room is full of shadow. She can't even see the far wall. Maybe there is no wall. The room seems to dissolve into darkness at the edges.

The smell of death is overpowering. The air feels greasy. Teresa covers her mouth with her sleeve, takes shallow breaths.

"Come on now," Kyle says. He looks like he did in the video. He looks real. Alive. "Don't be a little bitch about this. Don't be like the others." He gestures at the far corner of the room, but Teresa sees nothing there but darkness. "I can help you, just like you helped me. I'll get everyone in the world to watch you."

"Why?" Teresa chokes out. "Why me?"

"You deserve way more views than you've been getting," he says, turning back to the computer, typing something. He sounds matter-of-fact, entirely casual. "You've got actual talent. And you're pretty, but you don't try too hard. You don't shove it in people's faces. You're real, you know. Not like the others. You can be way bigger than Brick ever was."

"You killed him," Teresa says. Her heartbeat is pounding in her ears. She feels dizzy.

Kyle shrugs, dismissive. He turns to look at her again. "He killed himself, really. All I wanted was for him to acknowledge me, to know that he'd hurt me and to feel sorry. For his viewers to know me, too. Maybe get a little of what I deserved, finally. You can understand that, right? You would have done the same thing."

"No," says Teresa, and she means to sound defiant, but it comes out sounding weak, uncertain. She'd often wished she could change places with Brick. Of course she had.

"You would," says Kyle, his voice louder for a moment. Assertive. Almost angry. "You're just like me. You understand what it feels like to be stuck in a tiny room. To be powerless. Only able to watch."

Teresa wants him to shut up, to stop telling her what she's like, what she'd do, what she understands.

But what if he's right?

She used Brick for views, didn't she, even if she told herself that she was only doing it for his own good. What if, on some level, she and Kyle are the same? Two small, stuck people, two parasites, unable to live their own lives.

"Let me control the body," Kyle says, returning his attention to the screen. "It will be much easier that way."

He turns up the volume.

A drumbeat, coming out of the computer speakers.

No, a heartbeat.

Her heartbeat. It stops, misses a beat. Starts again.

 **Replay is live now with 2 viewers, at least**
CATEGORY: Mind Game

We are seeing through her eyes. Through her body's eyes.

There is not much to see. A wall, a floor.

The edges of the screen are blurry, peripheral.

The view shifts.

We are seeing the left hand. It trembles. One finger twitches. A quick flutter.

The view shifts.

Someone else is in the room. We hear her voice. "Replay? Teresa?"

The view slowly turns. We see the room now. A girl with white-blond hair is watching us. She is moving closer, she is peering right at us.

Does she see us, in here?

We try to speak, but it doesn't work. We are muted. We try to move, but we cannot.

We do not have the appropriate permissions.

20://

On the computer screen, Teresa can see the view from her body's eyes jostling around, bouncing from wall to ceiling. She can see her arm hanging limply, draped over Ozma's shoulder. It looks like she's being carried. Where is Ozma taking her?

Kyle is pressing keys, spam-clicking the mouse. On the screen, Teresa's arm moves. He is trying to get control, just like he did with Brick.

Teresa thinks of Lil. Of what Kyle must have made Brick do to her when she tried to intervene, tried to stop the stream.

He's going to hurt Ozma. He's going to make Teresa hurt Ozma.

Her friend. Her magnificent friend. All her fault. Again.

Teresa screams. A scream of rage, for once, instead of fear. She grabs the only object in the room, that dusty trophy, and runs at him, flight giving way to fight, some primal violence rising inside of her. She lifts it high, brings it down hard against the back of his head, right at the spot where the hair swirls, that little tender patch of scalp.

The trophy hits with a crunch.

Kyle's skull cracks.

Like an eggshell. It splinters. Caves in. He falls forward onto the desk.

The back of his head is gaping, open. The inside wet and glistening. A meaty pink. Oozing watery blood.

Teresa drops the trophy. She feels faint with shock. It shouldn't have broken through his skull like that. She's not that strong. She can see his brains. She killed him. She didn't mean to kill him. She never meant to kill anyone.

And yet she keeps doing it, doesn't she?

She killed Becks, her best friend. She killed Steven, the driver. Not with her own hands, sure, but it was her fault. They would both be alive if it weren't for her.

Kyle was right. They are the same. She's a murderer, a monster.

On the computer screen, she sees the dashboard of a car, the view from the passenger's seat. Is Ozma taking her to the hospital? Teresa doesn't think that will do any good. Ozma should leave her behind. She should run far away before she gets hurt, too.

Kyle's body starts to shake. Then a sound, a wet rasp. It gets louder. His body shakes more.

And Teresa realizes he is laughing.

Of course. He's dead already. He's a ghost. She is a fool. A terrified, desperate fool who is going to die, too, and who probably deserves it.

Kyle sits up, turns around, and it isn't him anymore. Isn't a young man in a gray T-shirt with unkempt hair, with circles under his eyes, with patchy stubble on his cheeks.

He's just shadow. A figure made of darkness, darker than the dim room. Two pinpoints of light for eyes. Searing blue-white, like the light of a screen, like the glowing rectangles but sharpened, condensed. It pierces her, that light.

Let go. The voice is in her head. It's in her bones.

She falls back onto the floor, her muscles suddenly weak. The trophy lies beside her, still slick with blood, a gobbet of something unspeakable clinging to the handle. She can just barely read the text etched into the side: *Second place, fifty-meter dash.* She pulls herself to her hands and knees and crawls away, across the dusty floor.

The dust is everywhere. The white dust. Piled up in the corners, coating every surface. It is moving, though there is no breeze here, the air stagnant as a swamp. The dust is writhing.

It is moving toward her. It is surging. Swarming.

It is not dust anymore, but maggots. Thousands of them, smaller than grains of rice, but moving together. She staggers to her feet, tries to run, but they reach her quickly, piling up around her feet. She stomps them. Their bodies pop and burst. She can feel it even through the rubber soles of her sneakers.

Kyle is watching her from his chair, impassive. He looks like himself again, but the room seems darker than before, shadows pooling in every corner.

Teresa realizes that the darkness is moving, too. It surges toward her just like the maggots, but faster. Tiny black insects this time. Right out of her nightmares, her childhood memory. Their legs make a whispering, hushing sound as they swarm. Almost like rain.

She screams, tries to run.

But they reach her, and unlike the maggots, they climb. She can see them clearer now. They are ants, big, fat, glistening black ones, with sharp mouthparts. They scale her jeans with ease. Some slip beneath and she can feel the tickling brush of their tiny legs, just like when she was six, but worse this time. So much worse. She tries to shake them off, flailing, frantically swatting at her clothes. Her foot skids on the gooey residue of smashed maggot corpses and she falls to the ground.

Insect bodies crunch beneath her. She pushes herself back up, but the ants are on her hands now, on her arms, covering her skin like gloves.

They bite her. She tries to brush them off, but they stick to her, and she only succeeds in dragging their sharp mandibles across her skin. Small cuts open all down her arms, stinging and bleeding.

The ants squirm inside the cuts, wriggling deeper, under her skin, like splinters.

"Stop!" she cries. "Please!"

Their small dark bodies move under her skin. She feels them digging deeper, wriggling through muscle. They are all over her, coating her arms and legs and torso, scuttling, slicing, burrowing in.

Kyle has gotten up from his chair. He is standing over her now, looking down.

"It didn't have to be this way," he says.

She doesn't scream, but only because they've reached her face now. They are sliding over her lips. They are pushing, trying to get inside her mouth. She squeezes her eyes shut, but they are slipping under her lids. They are pressing against the surface of her eyes.

She is not a person anymore. Just a container for fear and pain.

"Let go," says Kyle, for the last time.

REC ▶

Our view is from the dashboard, phone
mounted in some kind of holder, tilted toward
Ozma. She sits in the driver's seat, one hand
on the wheel, the other moving back from the
phone.

"I'm making this video as evidence."

She keeps her eyes on the road as she speaks.
Out the windows, we can see trees, an ocean of
green.

"In case something happens. In case
we don't make it."

The roads are narrow and twisty, curving one
way and then the other. Ozma slows on the
turns, then speeds up, then slows.

"Maybe I shouldn't even have brought this,
I don't know. I kept it off until now. We're far
enough into the mountains that there's
no cell service. No radio either."

She reaches out, presses a button on the
dashboard, turns a knob. Static fuzzes out, too
loud. She turns it off.

"We came here once on a field trip when I was a kid. The quiet zone. There's a bunch of telescopes in the middle of it and there's laws or something, so the signals won't interfere with the readings. They are looking at things way out far in the universe. Black holes and shit. And aliens. I mean, they aren't looking at aliens yet, as far as I know, but they're looking for them. They showed us a slideshow on the field trip and let us look up close at one of the smaller telescopes. So I'm hoping it's safe. I'm hoping this will save her."

She glances to the side, at the passenger seat. We can't see what's there.

"I'm rambling. If anyone finds this, you need to disconnect your phone, turn off the Wi-Fi. All those people who are possessed, that's the way to save them. My friend Replay, she—"

A hand comes into view suddenly, from the side. Not Ozma's. It must be the passenger. The hand makes a grab for the wheel.

"Jesus Christ!"

A quick struggle. The car veers. Ozma pushes
the hand away.

"Stop it! What are you doing?"

The passenger comes into view, lunging over to
Ozma's side, reaching for the wheel again.

The car swerves violently. The phone is knocked
loose from its holder. A blur of green through
the window.

And then darkness.

21://

Teresa lets go. She can feel herself moving further from her body, detaching, leaving the pain and fear behind.

"There you go." She hears Kyle's voice, as if from a distance, from underwater. "Isn't that better?"

She can see herself, now, her body, or at least the shape of it, down there on the floor, buried under a roiling blanket of insects.

She can see other things down there, too, huddled shapes in the farthest, darkest corners of the room. Bodies.

She can't tell if they are asleep or dead. One of the bodies has a head that's shaped wrong.

Kyle has returned to his computer. On the screen Teresa can see the view from the car. See her own arms—her body's arms—reaching for the wheel.

She is far from herself, so far. Far from the ants, from Kyle. Far from feelings. Drifting farther by the moment, up and away. She could just keep going. It would be so easy. So peaceful. The darkness up here is velvety soft, a summer's night sky. There are even stars, twinkling gently.

Or no, not stars. *Eyes.*

Millions of eyes, without face or lid or lash. They float in the void. Little disembodied orbs with dark pupils. Some are so close that she can see their irises, blue and brown and green. The darkness is thick with them, as crowded as a swarm of gnats. Their glistening surfaces reflect the dim light of the computer screen far below. They seem to be watching it.

On that small distant screen, the car is swerving off the road. The view jerks back and forth. Hands grip the wheel while another set of hands tries to pry them away.

Ozma.

Teresa is so far gone, she can barely grasp at the name, but she finds it. Ozma. In the real world, she is in a car with Ozma. A girl she cares about so much. A girl she thinks she might love. And they are going to crash. They are going to die.

No.

No.

No. Not again. She can't let it happen again.

With a horrible, wrenching effort, Teresa jerks herself back into connection, back into her body. It hurts so much. But she does it. She feels the ants, writhing all over her. She feels the sharp pain, the burning agony as they burrow deep into her muscles, biting and tearing.

She thinks of what her therapist told her about grief, which is just another form of pain. She doesn't try to escape this feeling. She feels it. She accepts it. She opens herself up to it.

And then for an instant, she is in her true body again, in the car.

She yanks her arms away from the wheel, shoves herself back into the passenger seat. Branches smack against the windshield, scraping the glass with a high-pitched shriek.

Teresa allows herself a moment of joy as she beholds the face of Ozma, who is gritting her teeth and swearing as she jerks the wheel to the side and pulls the car back onto the road. Teresa tries to speak, but she can't open her mouth. She feels heavy, drugged.

She feels herself falling backward, into the seat and then further.

With a *thump* she lands on her ass on the floor in Kyle's small dark room.

"You bitch," he spits.

The ants are gone. Or no, not gone. They've all made their way inside her now. She can still see them, though they've lost their shape. They are just dark shadows, moving under the surface of her skin. An itch she can't scratch.

She won't let herself give in to panic. She tries to will herself back into her true body again, but it's not that easy. Still, she knows now that she is not entirely powerless.

She pushes herself up to her feet. She feels terribly weak, worn out from fighting. The ghost is draining her, she thinks, using her up like a battery. He's focused on his computer screen now, typing furiously.

She staggers to the corner of the room, the place where she'd seen the bodies before. There's not even a proper floor over here. The musty carpet simply breaks apart, like a digital glitch, dissolving into noise and then shadow.

She finds the first body, recognizes it easily. Black hair. High cheekbones. KingCoal.

He's lying on his back and he's not dead. His eyes turn slowly toward her.

"We need to fight him," she says, kneeling beside him. "We need to get control back."

His voice is a ragged, whispery rasp. "What do you think I've been doing?" He tries to sit up, but his arms shake and he collapses back down. His breathing is shallow. Each inhale seems to pain him. "I'm so tired."

He's been possessed much longer than she has. Perhaps this is the fate that awaits her, slowly dying in a dark corner, discarded and powerless. There are other bodies in the shadows beyond him, huddled forms of people Teresa doesn't recognize. Other streamers, maybe. Brick isn't here. These people are all still alive, but barely. When she tries to rouse them, they groan and cover their faces, or simply lie there motionless.

Teresa finds Horsegirl and tries to pull off their rubber mask, but it seems to be stuck. She takes their hand instead, squeezes it.

"Come on," she says. "We can get through this."

Teresa glances up. The eyes are there, just visible in the darkness. She thinks they must be the paralyzed viewers, their mute regard giving Kyle power.

What can she do? How can she save them? How can she save herself?

Horsegirl's hand spasms and clenches, their fingers digging painfully into Teresa's palm. They begin to shake all over. A wet, phlegmy groan comes from within the mask. Teresa tries frantically to pull it off again, but she sees now that it is fused with their skin, a seamless transition from shoulder to rubber.

"Stay with me," Teresa shouts. "Hold on."

"Give up."

Teresa spins around. Kyle is standing there, though he looks less substantial than he did before. His face is all shadow, his eyes shining with the strange, piercing light.

Horsegirl's body contorts once more and then goes abruptly still. Their hand slips from Teresa's grip.

They begin to fade.

"No," says Teresa. "No, come back!" She tries to grab on to Horsegirl, but their body dissolves into darkness. Teresa grasps at nothing.

They're gone.

"If you fight," Kyle says, "you'll just burn yourself out faster."

"Stop this," Teresa says. She wants to hit him again, to hurt him, but she doesn't think it would help. Maybe she can get through to him somehow. "Please. Let us go."

It isn't fair that he's the one who gets to live on after death. If that text conversation had been real instead of a trick, if Becks had lived on, if they'd had even one more minute together . . . Teresa could have said goodbye, she could have told Becks how much she loved her, how much she would carry their friendship—the pain and the joy both—with her forever.

And Becks—what would she say?

Teresa would have given anything to find out.

"You're wasting this chance," she tells Kyle. "You're wasting your time with us. We don't matter. Let us go. You should reach out to the people who loved you."

"No one loved me," he says, his voice like a vise, squeezing all the air from the room. The darkness itself seems to be pressing in.

Teresa feels suddenly claustrophobic. She wants fresh air. She wants out. She squeezes her eyes shut. For a moment, she sees a flash of green. Sunlight strobing through the trees.

"You can struggle all you want," Kyle says. She opens her eyes and she's back in the dark room, the smell of rot and death wrapping around her. "It won't do any good. You'll just die like the others."

"I'm sure people cared about you," Teresa says, gasping to breathe through the thick air, desperate. Are her own parents worried about her? Is Jason all right? She wishes she could talk to them now. Tell them she's sorry. "What about your friends, your family, your mom or dad? Did you have any siblings?"

"I don't remember."

"You don't remember?" Is he messing with her? She can't read his expression. His tone is flat.

"I remember this," Kyle says. He points behind him, at the desk and the computer, a cold white rectangle of light in the darkness. The screen is still showing the view from her body, the trees rushing past on a rural road. At the very least she can try to keep him distracted, buy Ozma more time.

"Do you remember anything about your life?" she asks. "Real stuff. Like track. You must have been good at that. You won a trophy. Do you remember running? Being outside?"

"I don't remember any of that," Kyle says. There's a funny edge to his voice, almost a quaver. Like maybe he wishes he does.

This isn't really Kyle, is it?

This isn't his spirit or his soul or whatever it is that makes a person who they are. This is just what got left behind after he died. What got left online.

"You're not him," she says.

Kyle's face—the ghost's face—twists into a scowl. Strange light burns in his eyes. His features blur.

He can't remember his life because he never lived it. He's never been anywhere beyond this dark little room with no edges, made only of those parts of Kyle's real room that could be seen on his stream. He's just a reflection in a screen. A shadow.

"Whatever," the ghost says, voice gone hollow, echoing, empty. "If you won't give me what I want, I'll find someone else. There are so many people watching me now."

Teresa looks up at the void overhead. The eyes are still there. Silent, staring down at them.

"They are watching the clips you posted," the ghost says. "They are watching the streams."

She notices something odd, then. The eyes are blinking out. Going dark. A few at first, and then as she watches, more and more. They are vanishing from the black sky. Shutting but never opening. Dying?

"There's a new trend," says the ghost. He doesn't look human at all anymore. He's pure shadow, with eyes of burning light. "A new challenge. People are filming themselves opening as many doors as they can. They want to see if I show up. And believe me, I'm showing up. I'm everywhere."

There were more eyes in the sky than Teresa could even dream of counting before. Millions maybe.

But now if she had to guess she'd say there are only a few hundred.

The ghost notices, finally, his own blazing eyes following her gaze upward.

The eyes are blinking out faster and faster. Now there are only a hundred or so.

Now there are a few dozen.

The ghost screams, but not with a human voice. It sounds like a blast of static.

He launches himself at Teresa. His hands reach for her throat and squeeze.

"What have you done?" he shouts, but she can't answer. She can't breathe. She looks to the eyes, as if they could help her.

Now there are only three.

Now there are none.

We can't see her anymore. The princess in the mirror.

She has driven deep into the Monongahela, the national forest. We cannot see through the trees, which grow so thickly over the mountain they look like one entity, one green-furred beast.

We get only the briefest, barest glimpses. Her phone has tumbled to the floor of the car, but it is not the angle that prevents us from seeing. This is the quiet zone. No service here. The car passes through a town, speeds by a house with Wi-Fi. The signal is weak, but it reaches the road for an instant. A flash.

The car turns and turns and turns around a sharp curve lined with yellow arrow signs. They are going too fast. A coin slides back and forth in the cup holder. The centrifugal force presses the other girl, the dark-haired one, sideways against the door.

We see tilted power line poles. The red spike of a church. A blue tin roof.

We lose her again. No signal.

He wasn't lying when he said there were others. He is not the only one here in this place that is not a place. The place that is nowhere and everywhere.

There are many of us.

We are watching what he has done with interest. We are not ourselves anymore, of course, and neither is he, but he seems to be
holding on harder than we have. We are just data now. We are
images, impressions.

Another flash. We see the car spinning wildly around a curve. A
gnarled guardrail, never replaced after an old impact. Ahead, a
break in the trees. Layered mountains in the distance, colors flat-
tened by the atmosphere. They look like sheets of cut paper in
receding shades of green and blue.

We are watching you, too. We can get inside your outline, the
shape you have made for us with the questions you ask and the
pictures you post, the things you buy, the things you watch. The
shape of your gaze, the shape of your desire. Not quite a full person but enough to get an idea of you. A ghost of you.

That is all we are. The outlines left behind.

We were just like you once. We scrolled. We fell down rabbit holes.
We once at 3 a.m. searched "am i dying?" and we were.

One last flash—the car careens off the road, down a paved drive,
past low buildings, enormous filtration ponds lined with black
tarps, a water tower. The drive ends in a barrier arm, striped white
and red. The car crashes through, skids.

And then we lose her for good.

22://

Teresa is in the car. She is choking, writhing in the seat. Her hands flail out and hit the glass of the passenger side window. The car fishtails.

She is in the dark room, the ghost's shadowy hands around her throat.

She is in the car. A sound like an explosion. Her head slams forward. A flash of white. A deer? No. The airbag. A smell she remembers from somewhere. Acrid smoke.

She is in the dark room. Kyle's ghost is screaming. He lets go. She drops to the ground.

The car. Ozma is shouting something, but the words are muffled. She's opening the door. She's dragging Teresa out of the car.

The dark room. Except it's not even really a room anymore. The musty carpet and the dresser are gone. All that's left is the desk, sitting in the middle of the darkness. Kyle himself is hunched over in front of it. He is frantically refreshing the page.

Teresa coughs and gasps. She crawls forward until she is close enough to see the screen, to read the words in the center of it.

No internet

Try:
- Checking the network cables, modem, and router

- Reconnecting to Wi-Fi
- Running Windows Network Diagnostics

Kyle turns. His face is human again, but ghostly pale in the light of the screen.

"It isn't fair," he says, and he sounds almost like a child. A little boy. Lost and afraid.

"It isn't," she says, and she means it differently now. Kyle got a few more years of life than Becks did, but he still died very young. He died while he was trying, desperately, to reach out to the world, to connect. She'll never know the real Kyle now. The ghost he left behind is only the smallest, saddest part of him. That's not fair at all.

Teresa knows what it is like to be stuck in the worst part of your own mind, stuck in a loop of dark thoughts. What would her own ghost be made of? Frantic refreshing. Fearful searches. Obsession and isolation.

Kyle looks like he might cry. Teresa feels sorry for him. She really does. She remembers what Ozma said about the people who sent her cruel messages. How being so full of hate must eat them from the inside.

Kyle's expression twists suddenly.

"This is all your fault," he says, vicious and angry again.

He throws himself at her once more, knocks her off her feet. They fall backward together, hit the ground hard enough to send pain shooting all through her body.

The ground isn't darkness, though.

It's grass.

Teresa is on her back, staring up at the sky. She hears the whistle of a far-off train. The sound is strange, haunting and breathy, like a human voice singing.

Someone is dragging her by the legs.

Stop. Kyle's voice inside her head. He closes her eyes. She can feel him doing it, another person controlling her body. She struggles against his will, forces her eyes back open.

"Help," she tries to say to Ozma, but it comes out only as a strangled moan.

Kyle jerks Teresa's left arm up to her own face. Her arm no longer belongs to her. It scratches against her cheek. It scrabbles and grasps. It is reaching for her eye.

A fingernail scrapes across her cornea. Teresa screams, finally breaking through Kyle's control just long enough to yank the hand away. Tears flood her vision, turning the world into a watercolor wash of smeared shape and color.

Ozma has stopped dragging her. She drops to her knees in the grass, bends over her.

"Teresa! What's going on?"

To her horror, Teresa feels her left hand reaching out for Ozma. The hand grabs Ozma's wrist, digs its fingernails in hard. Ozma shouts in surprise, in pain.

"No!" With a burst of adrenaline, of absolute panic—her worst fears realized—Teresa finds her voice again. She grabs her own left hand with her right hand, pulls it away. She can't hurt Ozma. She won't.

"Shit," says Ozma, sounding on the verge of crying herself. "What do I do? I thought maybe bringing you here would be enough."

Teresa blinks her own tears away. For the first time, she notices the enormous telescope standing sentinel across the grass from them, gleaming white. It looks like an oversized science fair toothpick project, improbable against the dark trees.

"Run," she tells Ozma, her voice still weak and strangled-sounding. "Get away from me."

But Ozma doesn't do it. She reaches for Teresa's hand instead, the left one, and she grasps it firmly between her own, stilling it, holding it. Teresa feels the warmth of Ozma's palm, feels all the miraculous bones. Kyle wants to crush them, but she won't let him do that.

Kyle is still in her head, but it seems like she's in his now, too. She feels his desperation, his loneliness. He is the harsh white glow of the screen at night, the links that lead nowhere, the cold comments of strangers. He is video after video of people fucking up, people hurting each other. Comment threads of people hating everyone, hating themselves. *You are ugly, you are useless, you were doomed from birth. The world doesn't want you. Nobody wants you. We are all laughing at you. Your weak chin. Your thin limbs. You are without value, without hope. No one will ever love you. No one will ever touch you. You were a mistake. A failure. A stain. Just fucking end it.*

Teresa sees what it was like for Kyle's ghost at the very beginning. Locked in that small, dark place that wasn't even quite a room. Watching Brick, seething at his effortless grace, his popularity, his confidence. At first the ghost could only watch. He kept trying to type in the chat, trying to reach out, to be seen, to connect with someone, anyone.

He was small and angry and alone. So alone.

Teresa wants to fight him, but she doesn't know how. He has jealousy, hatred, resentment. What does she have?

Fear?

Kill yourself, he says inside her head, and it echoes back to her with a thousand voices, all of them screaming. Teresa is shaking with the effort of fighting herself, fighting Kyle. She is spasming, seizing. Pain explodes through her body, her muscles trying to tear themselves apart, pulled in different directions by the two of them as they wrestle for control.

"Shit shit *shit*," Ozma is saying. "Stay with me, Teresa. Please don't die."

Teresa is in so much pain that she wants to die. She wants to let go again, wants to give up, to run away from all of this. What's the point of living in a world so dark and full of hate? What is the point of living when it hurts so much?

But there is a tiny voice in the corner of her mind telling her to hold on. It is soft at first, nearly inaudible, but it is getting louder.

There is light in the darkness, the voice says. Teresa says. The voice is her. It's just her. The part of her that doesn't want to give up talking to the part of her that does.

There is good out there, too, if you know where to look. Funny words. Cute cats. Unexpected connections. People being kind. People laughing together, grieving together, working together. Sending each other memes. Did you know that inside you there are two wolves? One is gay and the other is gay. And yes the world is bad and hard and my best friend died too young. She was alive once, a full, real wonderful person, and then something broke in the delicate machine of her body and she was gone. That was it. Her time was over. It wasn't fair and it will never be fair and there is nothing I can do about it except continue to love her and to love the world, in all its horror and its wonder, because if I had died instead of her, I would want her to keep living. I would want her to experience everything, the pain and the joy both. Look at this world. Look at these mountains, those wisps of mist clinging to the hollows. Look at the telescope, the labor that went into building it, the optimism that there is more out there than we've been able to see before. It is listening to the sky. Reaching deep into the darkness. Trying to find a voice out there. A connection. Isn't that something? The unbearable hope of it all?

Kyle sees the telescope. She can feel him seeing it, yearning toward it, reaching for it across the distance. She can feel him stretching himself thin, holding on to her mind but at the same time pushing himself into the telescope itself.

He thinks it is a way back to power, to control. He thinks he can transmit himself through it, reach people's screens again. Get back those views he thought he deserved. Get revenge on a world he felt wronged him, cast him aside, ignored him, left him alone to rot in a small dark room.

But this is a tool built not to broadcast but to listen, so sensitive it can hear things many lightyears away. It is listening to pulsars, to supernovas, to the black hole at the center of our galaxy.

Kyle's ghost has made it into the telescope, into its delicate inner workings. He is possessing the fine machinery, the sensors and reflectors. He is hearing all the things it can hear. Hearing the shapes of distant galaxies. Hearing how much bigger this world is than one small dark room, one small bright screen.

Oh, he says, and she feels it too. She feels his surprise, his awe, feels his grip on her weaken, the pain in her body receding.

He is made of hate and sorrow, defined by the worst of what this world has to offer, the worst of what Kyle was given. But maybe there's a way forward, even for him.

Oh, he says again, but fainter. He is letting go. He is dissolving. The shadowy figure and his pinprick eyes like stars. He is becoming night sky. He is becoming something new, something bigger and stranger than he was before. The final thread snaps.

Teresa's body lies in the grass.

"Teresa?"

She feels weak, hollowed out.

Empty.

"Is it you?" Ozma asks. She stares down at Teresa, her eyes wet with tears. She looks rumpled, her hair flying in every direction. Smears of mud streak across her sweatshirt, her cheek.

"It's me," says Teresa. "It's me."

It is raining. Only lightly, the raindrops little sparks on Teresa's skin, lighting her up, making her feel real, reminding her of her own body.

"He's gone," she says. She's not certain where he's gone, if he moved on to some other realm, or if he's still out there. But he's gone from her head, from her body. They belong to her once more.

She sits up, crawls to Ozma, wraps her arms around her. "You saved my life," she says.

Ozma hugs her back. "Just repaying the favor."

They kiss. The rain slides down their faces. Teresa leans back to push her wet hair out of her eyes and from the corner of her vision she spots a dark shape about fifty feet away, emerging from the trees.

She tenses, ready to run or to fight.

But it's not a shadowy figure. Not a person at all.

A black bear. Trundling along the grass as casually as an oversized dog, belly swinging. Two small cubs trot close behind her.

Teresa and Ozma hold very still, watching. The bears pass by the telescope, cross the open grass, and plunge back into the pines.

"It's so beautiful here," Teresa says.

"It really is."

Teresa reaches instinctively for her pocket, her phone. "Oh," she says, catching herself. Her phone is far, far away. "I was going to take a picture."

"I guess we can just remember it," says Ozma.

Teresa is sure she will remember it for the rest of her life. This moment is perfect. She tries to memorize every detail. The rain and the mountains and Ozma there beside her.

Maybe later, when everything is back to normal, she will make a post about how good it feels, finally, to truly disconnect.

She digs her fingers deep into the wet grass, and she laughs.

EPILOGUE

||||||||||||

Replay is live now with 34.2K viewers
Category: Just Chatting
LIVE REACTING TO SPOOKY VIDEOS YOU SUBMIT

Replay sits in their room, in a high-end gamer chair, white with silver accents. Behind them on the wall is a neon sign, pink and purple, spelling out their name in glowing loops.

Their hair is short, shaved on the sides. The points of their black eyeliner are sharp enough to cut.

"Alrighty then, my little Replayers, that's about all I've got in me for today."

Chat

[1:05:02]—no don't go!
[1:05:03]—aw I only just joined
[1:05:04]—Replay staaaay

There is an overlay for subscriber count, ticking up by the moment. Another overlay with links to social media alongside a small cartoon depiction of Replay and the words "any pronouns."

"But no need to despair. I'll stream again tomorrow. And don't forget I'm doing an IRL collab with Ozma in two weeks."

[1:05:09]—omg yes
[1:05:10]—can't wait
[1:05:10]—they are the absolute cutest I ship it so hard
[1:05:11]—r they officially dating?

"I'm so excited. We have a lot of things planned."

[1:05:14]—yah Ozma confirmed it last month
[1:05:15]—couple goals FR

We can see the bedroom door behind them, but it is closed.

"And hopefully, if all goes well in a few months, we'll be living in a streamer house together, along with Jolley and RnBw."

[1:05:20]—catjam
[1:05:20]—call it haus of gay
[1:05:21]—living the DREAM

Replay grins.

"You all are seriously not ready! There's going to be. So. Much. Content."

Teresa is sitting in her room, in her fancy new chair, in the glow of the neon sign. She is by herself, but she isn't alone.

She never streams alone now.

Brick is here.

He is standing behind her, uncomfortably close. Closer than he usually stands. His hands are on the back of her new chair. His hair is perfect, not a strand out of place. He doesn't speak. He never speaks. Most of the time he just stares at her or at the camera, impassive. Sometimes he smiles, but the expression looks awkward and halting. As if he isn't quite used to having a face.

It's not really Brick, of course. It's his ghost. His echo. The digital imprint he left behind. Brick died while he was streaming, just like Kyle, so it makes sense that he, too, would linger on after death. Teresa isn't sure why he's haunting her in particular. Maybe he feels a connection since they were both possessed. Either that, or he blames her somehow. She tries not to think about that too much.

Behind him, the room is crowded.

Lil is here, too, and KingCoal and Hedgelord and Horsegirl— masked forever in death. They stand behind Brick, all of them watching her. Behind them are others, smaller streamers and viewers who died after being possessed. Teresa has learned the names of some of them from news articles and posts made by bereaved friends and family. And behind them there are still others, less distinct. She doesn't know who they are.

But they are here now. Shadowy figures in the background of all Replay's streams, only visible on the screen. They don't show up to the viewers. When Teresa watches the VOD back, when she posts the video, it will look like she is alone. As far as she can tell, she's the only one who can see them.

She opened the door once, and it seems she can never close it again.

These ghosts don't act like Kyle. They aren't trying to break through, aren't trying to possess her.

Or at least they haven't tried, yet.

Teresa has tried muting her stream and talking to them, but they never respond. Most of the time they just watch her. Sometimes one will dart forward and she will flinch, and the chat will see her flinching at nothing and they will lose their collective mind. They live for that shit.

Now, she ends stream. Her grin slides abruptly away as she drops character.

In the beginning, the ghosts would disappear when the stream was over, but lately they've begun to linger even after the camera is off. She can see them, very faintly, reflected in the monitor's surface. She shuts down the computer and drapes a towel over the monitor, so she can't see the screen.

She's just Teresa, now, not Replay. It's become more and more jarring to make that switch. Sometimes Replay feels like the real one, and Teresa the persona.

Replay uses *they/them* pronouns, but it's not really *they* singular. It's *they* plural. When Replay says, "I can't believe we've hit ten thousand subscribers!" they mean *me and all the ghosts*.

Teresa hasn't changed pronouns in everyday life. She thinks of herself as *she* with an asterisk, a footnote. She[1]* has time to figure

---

1   *But only sort of, only sometimes, only in certain moods.

it out. Maybe Teresa will switch to *they* eventually, maybe just *she/they*, or maybe even try out *he*, see how that feels for a while. Ozma called Teresa *my boyfriend* the other day, half-joking, and it gave her a flood of unexpected joy.

Anyway, Replay is the important one now. Teresa can wait in the background for a while, in the shadows, while Replay is on the rise.

She streams five days a week, on a regular schedule. She's a partner. She has sponsors. The Brick stuff catapulted her into the spotlight. In the aftermath of the possession, as Teresa tried to piece her life back together, she became the primary source for everyone out there who wanted to understand what happened. People were confused and scared. They were hungry for an explanation, for closure, solace. And she owed it to them, didn't she? She made a few short videos, and then when her account got unbanned, she decided she'd try a short stream.

The viewers poured in. More than she'd expected. More than she'd ever had before. More than she'd ever dared dream about. The kind of numbers that Brick used to pull.

And from the very first stream, he was there. Brick. His ghost.

She'd nearly passed out when she first spotted him standing by her bedroom door, but he didn't do anything threatening. He just stood there, watching her. And then the next time she streamed, he was there again. And then the time after that, Lil was with him. And the time after that . . .

Maybe she should have stopped after that first stream. Maybe she should never have started up again. She did try, a few weeks in, to take a break. She posted an announcement on all her socials, said her channel was going on a temporary hiatus.

The ghosts didn't like that.

Her monitor started glitching out, lines of broken pixel noise darting across the screen, jagged shards of color and light. Programs closed themselves. Her broadcasting software opened without prompting. When she stayed off her computer entirely, the glitchy lines moved to her phone. When she shut her phone off, the smart fridge downstairs acted up, the display flashing on and off at all hours. Her father had to unplug it.

As soon as she streamed again, everything calmed down. The fans were glad to have her back, too. She was rewarded with more subscribers, more followers, more views.

So, for now at least, for as long as people want to watch her, for as long as the ghosts remain peaceful, she will keep streaming.

Jason and her parents were both adamantly against it at first. They thought streaming was too dangerous. Her parents had read all the news reports about the mass catatonia, the deaths. They believed, as most people did, that the cause was psychological rather than supernatural. Jason knew the true story, knew that it was so much worse.

Teresa simply sat them all down and showed them how much money she was earning from subscribers and sponsors and that shut them up. She pays Jason sometimes to help manage the channel.

Now, Teresa puts on her noise-canceling headphones. She opens her bedroom door. She goes downstairs. She waves at her mom.

"Going to take a short walk," she says.

Her mom makes a slight involuntary move toward Teresa, as though she might try to hug her, or stop her. They did a few sessions of family therapy—all four of them—after she came home from West Virginia. Her parents had been beside themselves with worry the whole time, convinced she was dead, confused by Jason's explanation. Sometimes she thinks it's been harder for them to deal with the aftermath of that experience than it has been for her. She'd already had the worst thing in the world happen to her once before. She'd already been broken and put back together.

In the end, her mom simply gives her a tight smile. "Nice day for it," she says.

Teresa heads out the front door.

She can do that now. There's still a tug of anxiety every time she opens a door, every time she leaves the house, but she *does* leave the house. She makes a habit of doing it every day, trying to stay in practice. Her therapist is proud of her. He's helped her make a gradual plan of reintroduction to the places she couldn't go before. She takes it slow, letting herself acclimate to each new location. She can handle ten minutes in a grocery store now, though she prefers just going for short walks like this.

The sun is shining. The neighbor's yard is full of white and pink lilies, some of them almost as tall as Teresa. Blue cornflowers burst from cracks in the curb. They are almost too bright to stand. Things like that make her cry, sometimes. Sunlight through leaves. These tiny moments of beauty.

She keeps her head down, walking fast, avoiding other people, shifting nervously from foot to foot at the street crossing, waiting for the light. She pinches herself, hard. A reminder to stay in her body. Not to drift away.

She doesn't start to relax until she reaches the bottom of a dead-end street and the stone steps waiting there, set into a forested hillside, leading down to the river.

The trees grow thick here, their leaves blocking out all view of the city. She makes her way down, lets the green surround her, swallow her, obliterate all other thoughts.

The steps lead to a paved path that winds along the side of the river. Teresa walks, watching the trees sway, the sun dappling the pavement. Now and then, through the trees, she gets a glimpse of the river's gleaming surface, a gaggle of dozing geese on the bank, a lone duck drifting along the water's edge.

When Ozma visits, this is the first place Teresa wants to show her. She can almost picture it, the two of them walking the path, holding hands. Dating Ozma fills her with joy and terror in equal measure. She is terrified of losing her, of hurting her.

But isn't it worth it to try? She must stay true to the conviction she felt beneath the telescope that morning. Becks would want her to keep living, to open the door to all the horrible and wonderful possibilities of the world.

A jogger passes by with their smartphone in their hand. Teresa turns her head away, but not quite fast enough.

She still sees it.

A face, flashing quickly on the screen there and gone. A pair of eyes. Watching her.

She sees them everywhere she goes these days.

The library. The coffee shop. Computers, laptops, phones, the little touchscreen tablet the barista spins around for you to sign and tip, the self-checkout at the grocery store. Even in the blank face of her phone when she turns it off at night. Every single time she looks at a screen now, any screen, there's a good chance she'll see a face that shouldn't be there, a pair of eyes that don't belong, staring out at her.

That's us.

Do you see us, too?

Look harder, next time, in the reflection of a dark screen. Your computer, your phone, the little windows you surround yourself with. The little doors. We are there, I promise.

And we see you.

ACKNOWLEDGMENTS

| | | | | | | | | | | | | | | | | | | | |

Ultra-mega-platinum-diamond-tier thanks to top chatters Jim McCarthy, Jenny Bak, AZ Hackett, Steven Scaife, Nathan Willy, MK Klenkar, Brian Horrocks, Lucia Baez, Kelley Brady, Sola Akinlana, and everyone else who helped this book go live.